Of Introductions and Abductions

A Monkey Queen Adventure

.

Robert Dahlen

For Adelle,
with thanks and penguins.

Chapter One

It was another crappy Friday for Beth McGill. She had slept through her alarm, found a hole in her favorite Agatha Heterodyne t-shirt, painfully combed a snarl out of her past-her-shoulders-length brownish blonde hair, and swore when she saw that she had run out of strawberry jam for her toast. She barely made it to her first class on time, and was met with yet another disapproving stare from the TA. She hadn't had time to pack a lunch, so she had to settle for a decent but overpriced meal at the campus pizzeria. And she discovered that she'd forgotten to charge her smartphone and couldn't follow the updates from her webfriends who were attending the big convention, which made her feel bad all over again about not being able to afford to go. And which made the tomato sauce and grease stain on her jeans seem small.

Beth found herself wondering, again, if she had chosen the right college. She had wanted to get as far away from bickering parents and Midwest suburban life as possible, and Cooper College, a smallish campus in a smallish town tucked into the redwoods of northern California, had lured her with their curriculum, which focused on English and literary studies, and a generous scholarship. But no matter how she tried, she couldn't fit in with the other students. It seemed like no one else there had ever seen a fantasy movie or television show, let alone waited in line all day for the latest Tolkien film; no one else there had ever read a sci-fi or fantasy novel, never mind tried cosplaying as "Harriet Dresden".

She knew it didn't help that she dressed like a stereotypical geek girl. She always wore her green army jacket, faded jeans, black sneakers and whatever t-shirt she felt like putting on that morning. Her thick glasses tended to offset her bright blue eyes. And campus cuisine, and an overdependence on comfort food, had caused her to put on extra weight.

By the end of her last class, Beth had managed to work herself into a state of near-depression. But her mood had brightened afterward, when she ran into Puck on the quad.

Even by the standards of both liberal arts colleges and northern Californian ones, Puck was a bit odd. If he had actual first and last names, he kept them to himself. He was short, half a head shorter than Beth, bearded and balding, and he tended to act like he had seen it all and it still quietly amused him. He also wore socks with sandals; he said it was because his feet got cold otherwise, and fashion be hanged. He was Beth's favorite professor, and the one reason she was glad that she chose Cooper. Puck had taken a liking to her as well, and thankfully not in a way that would have been highly unethical but gotten her an A. She enjoyed his anecdotes about Shakespeare and Austen, and he seemed amused by her day-to-day travails.

The travail that tickled Puck the most was Beth's continuing bad luck with roommates. She had gone through more than she cared to remember since she had started at Cooper, including the one who had fled to Manhattan and become a body-paint performance artist, the one who had tried to blackmail the TA after a legendary frat party, the one who had eloped with the tribal chief from Fiji and the one who had signed with the Harlem Globetrotters. Her most recent roommate had just moved out after getting a six-figure book deal for her real true story about being abducted by aliens.

"Wasn't she on Jerry Springer?" Puck asked as they walked across the tree-lined quad. He and Beth were the only ones not in a hurry; students rushed past, heading back to their dorms or apartments to get ready for the weekend, followed by faculty members trying to beat the traffic.

"She was supposed to be," Beth said, "but she canceled at the last minute. That's when VH1 was trying to sign her to a reality show. I was ready to kick her out anyway."

"Why is that?"

"She spent the rent money on alien costumes and video editing software."

Puck chortled. "So, lass," he said, "was there something else you wanted to talk about?"

"How—" Beth caught herself. "I shouldn't be surprised, should I? You've always known me better than I've known myself."

"Debatable, but do continue."

"Professor..." Beth gathered her thoughts and wrapped her jacket tighter around her as a breeze sprung up. "Have you ever felt trapped? Stuck in a rut?"

"How so?"

"All I ever seem to do any more is go to class, watch TV, study and sleep. It feels like...like I don't have a life. Sometimes, I feel like life is leaving me out, having a big party while I sit on the couch and eat too many appetizers."

"Interesting analogy," Puck said.

"And what do I have to look forward to when I graduate? A dead-end job in an office surrounded by brainwashed wage zombies? Or teaching kids how to get into their own ruts? I mean, what's the point?" Beth stopped, blinked, and reached under her glasses to rub her eyes; the breeze had blown some dust into them.

Puck paused for a moment before he spoke. "You know, lass, most people wait until midlife to have a midlife crisis."

Beth barely managed to hold back a smile. "Professor..."

"Hush, lass." He laid a hand on her shoulder. "It's not unusual for us to feel trapped in our daily routines. I've felt that way myself at times. But it won't be that way forever."

Beth nodded and blinked again as Puck said, "There is one constant in life, and that is change." He paused. "Something wrong?"

Beth shook her head and pulled herself together. "I'm okay," she said. "Just had some dust in my eyes."

Puck nodded. "Of course," he said. "But I have to run; I need to meet with the department head in ten minutes."

"On a Friday?"

"He's buying the first round," Puck said. Beth smiled and nodded.

They exchanged quick goodbyes. As Puck walked away, Beth stared after him. She hadn't meant to startle him, but she had been startled herself, when she had blinked.

For a moment, Puck's appearance had changed. Beth hadn't been overly bothered by his eyes; even though they had seemed darker and deeper, they always seemed dark and deep anyway.

His ears looking as pointed as Elrond's? That bothered her.

On a nearby rooftop, a crouching figure in yellow, black and red watched Beth and Puck go their separate ways. She stood and wiped a dusty hand on her leg. "JACK-pot," she said with a grin.

As the sun set, Beth sat on a bench, arms on knees, staring at the ground, mind racing. "So," she said out loud to herself, "either I'm going crazy, or the Professor is turning into an elf. Maybe both."

Beth stood up and looked around. She had wandered along, lost in thought, after Puck's brief change, and had wound up in an unfamiliar part of campus. Across from the bench where she'd been sitting were two classroom buildings, both unused recently due to budget cuts and ongoing renovations. The ground in the alley between the buildings was covered in trash, and the breeze that blew through there was cold enough to raise goosebumps.

Beth shivered in the early evening chill. Then, her stomach growled. "I get the hint," she mumbled. "Time to grab a burrito."

"Why would you want to do that?"

Beth turned and saw a man with sunglasses and a scraggly beard standing by a lamppost. He was wearing a sleeveless black t-shirt, beat-up jeans, and a sleazy smile. "You should get something to eat instead," he said, walking up to her. He paused for a moment, as if he was trying to remember his next line, and then said, "Can I come with you?"

Beth's first thought was *Good grief.* "No," she said, keeping her voice level and calm.

The man seemed to be shocked by her answer. "Why not?"

"Because, frankly, you're nowhere near my type. And my day's been weird enough already." Beth started to walk away, hoping that he would get the hint.

That hope abruptly faded as the man reached out to grab her. "You're coming with me," he said.

Beth blinked, surprised and startled—

And the man's appearance changed. He was a foot taller, with fallow skin and grotesquely yellow eyes. His dark, greasy hair was tied up in a topknot. And his teeth, which matched his eyes, were all pointed and sharp.

Beth jerked away from the monster—troll? Ogre?—and ran away as fast as she had ever run, down the alley between the two buildings. Panic moved her, but in her fear, she didn't see the board on the ground in front of her. She tripped over it and fell hard.

She wasn't hurt, but the fall knocked the wind out of her. As she rolled over, gasping for breath, the ogre stood in the mouth of the alley. "Ha! I have you now!" he said. He laughed cruelly as he raised his fist.

That's when Beth noticed someone standing next to the ogre. She was slender and short, not much over five feet tall, in her late teens. She was Asian, Beth guessed Japanese, with brown eyes and ruffled, slightly messy black hair that came to just above her eyebrows in front and down to her collar in back. She was wearing a yellow karate-style jacket with red trim over a black t-shirt and leggings, and a red pillbox hat with a matching scarf that was just long enough to make Beth wonder how she kept from tripping over it. She held in one hand a wooden staff with gold tips; it was taller than she was. She had one fist in the air, mimicking the ogre. She was grinning.

"Now," the ogre said, pointing at himself, "you will come with me." The woman pointed at herself.

"If you do not," and the ogre clenched a fist; again, the woman did the same.

"You will be destroyed!" the ogre said.

"NOT!" the woman shouted.

The ogre finally realized there was someone next to him. He turned to face the woman, looming over her but visibly confused. She grinned back at him. "Monkey Queen!" he finally said, stepping back.

"Right the first time, Sunshine!" she said, her grin widening.

The ogre growled and grabbed a cracked two by four from the ground. "I will destroy you, Monkey Queen!" he bellowed.

"Oh, it's always the same, isn't it?" the woman said as the ogre charged. "I meet a new guy, and all he wants is to destroy me. Whatever happened to romance anyway?"

And with that, the Monkey Queen jumped in the air and kicked the ogre in the face.

He roared wordlessly and staggered back. She landed on her feet and said, "I know. It must be a shock. But can't you just picture it? Our first date?"

The ogre swung his makeshift club at her. She easily bent out of its way. "The two of us out on a moonlit night..." she said.

The ogre swung again. The Monkey Queen raised her staff with both hands and parried the blow. The board splintered, but the staff wasn't even scratched. "...The wind blowing through my hair and your ears..." she said.

The ogre growled and raised a fist the size of a bowling ball. "And you smile and eat the flowers you just bought for me," she said as she hit the ogre over the head with her staff.

As the ogre fell to his knees, holding his head and wincing in pain, the Monkey Queen said, "Well, maybe we should have dinner first. You okay over there?" she shouted to Beth.

"M-m-me?" Beth said, still trying to absorb what she had seen as she sat up.

"Well, I don't mean Sunshine there. Did you smell his breath?" The woman grimaced. "But you still haven't answered my—"

"Monkey Queen!"

She spun around and had just enough time to say "Uh-oh" before the ogre hit her.

She hit the ground hard, dropping her staff, and didn't move. The ogre roared in triumph. "The Monkey Queen was no match for me!" he said as he bent down to pick her up. "My mistress will be pleased."

As Beth watched, a small voice inside her head whispered, *He's not paying attention to you. Run while you can. Get away.* Another part of her said, *Don't move! Stay still! Maybe he'll forget about you and leave you alone.* But then she realized that both voices were being drowned out by the one that was shouting *Screw this!*, and that's when, to her surprise, she grabbed an empty soda bottle and threw it at the ogre. "Back off!" she yelled.

The bottle bounced off the ogre's head, and he turned to face her. Beth gasped, her heart racing, as he said with a sneer, "So you are brave after all. No matter." He took two steps towards Beth; she tried to back away as he said, "I was told to bring you in alive, but if you—"

"That's it!"

The Monkey Queen jumped to her feet and grabbed the surprised ogre by his shirt. "I try to be nice, and this is what I get?" she said as she lifted him over her head. "The date's off!"

She gave the ogre an airplane spin. "Oh well, it wouldn't have worked out anyway. After all, I am the Monkey Queen…and you're a dork." She threw the ogre head-first into the garbage cans. "That should do it," she said, picking up her staff. "Now, are you okay?"

Beth tried to put what she was thinking into words. "I—you—he—"

"I know," the Monkey Queen said with a nod. "Sunshine there was tougher than I thought. But you still haven't answered my—"

"Look out!" Beth shouted.

The Monkey Queen glanced over her shoulder. The ogre, sitting up amid the garbage cans, had pulled a dagger from his boot. "Die, Monkey Queen!" he said as he threw it at her.

"Do you mind?" she yelled as she swung her staff at the dagger. "We're trying to have a conversation here!" The staff struck the dagger and sent it flying back at the ogre, hilt first. Before he could react, the hilt hit him in the forehead. He toppled over, unconscious.

"Say goodnight, Sunshine! Now," the Monkey Queen said to Beth, "let's see if we can get this in a complete, coherent sentence: Are you all right?"

"Yes."

"That's a complete, coherent sentence?" The Monkey Queen grinned.

"Don't play semantics games with me," Beth said. "I'm an English major."

"Gotcha. Need a hand up?"

"Sure."

As the Monkey Queen helped Beth up, they could hear someone approaching. "Campus security," Beth whispered.

The Monkey Queen nodded and planted one end of her staff on the ground. She grasped the other end and wrapped her free arm firmly around Beth's waist, moving close to her. Beth's eyes widened as her feet left the ground.

Chapter Two

The Monkey Queen's staff had grown. In seconds, it had lifted its passengers to the roof of one of the nearby buildings, bending slightly to set them down gently. That done, it then shrunk back to its previous size, just in time to not be noticed by the two security staffers who had shown up. "You could have warned me," Beth said.

"Sorry," her companion said. "I didn't want to stick around for questioning."

"But what about the ogre?"

The Monkey Queen knelt by the edge of the roof and peeked over the side. "His seeming is back, and he's still out cold, so they'll probably think he's drunk. Let's hope they put him in the tank for the night."

"Seeming?"

"Shhh. Wait until they're gone."

After a few minutes, the ogre was led off by the security staffers. As soon as they had left, the Monkey Queen stood up. "Okay!" she said, extending a hand. "Time for introductions. I'm the Monkey Queen, but my friends call me Michiko."

"Beth McGill." They shook hands.

"Pleased to meet you, Beth! Now, I know you've got a lot of questions, so ask away!"

"There's something I wanted to say first," Beth said. Michiko nodded, and Beth gathered her thoughts. "Michiko…thank you for helping me out there. I don't know what that ogre wanted with me, but I'm sure it wasn't anything good, and you got me out of a jam, and…well, thanks." She smiled warmly.

To Beth's surprise, Michiko blushed and looked away. "Aw, you're welcome," she said. "Glad I could help."

"You know," Beth said, "I've never heard of a 'Monkey Queen' before…"

"Now you have!" Michiko said, grinning again.

"But I know about the Monkey King."

"Do tell!"

"Well…" Beth paused, digging into her memories. "He was Sun Wukong, a monkey with mystical powers who considered himself to be the Great Sage, Equal of Heaven. The gods of China brought him to Heaven and tried to recruit him, then tame him, then fight him. None of that worked out very well. It took Buddha himself to defeat him and imprison him under a mountain for 500 years.

"Finally, the goddess Kwan-Yin showed the Monkey King mercy. She freed him and ordered him to accompany a priest named Tripitaka on a sacred quest. They picked up two companions, Pigsy and Sandy, along the way, and they had many adventures and fought monsters and demons."

"Not bad!" Michiko said.

Beth grinned. "Hey, I aced Comparative Mythology and Folklore last semester."

"But you left something out."

"I did? Which part?"

"It's the part that gets left out of all the retellings," Michiko said. "It's the part where he helped save the world.

"It was about a thousand years ago. Magic was at its peak on Earth, and everyone from everywhere was out to take advantage of it, or just take it for themselves. A band of heroes, including the Monkey King, fought to defend the Earth, while its greatest magicians performed a ritual designed to rein in magic.

"It worked too well. Earth's magic was all but drained away. Many of the races and creatures that depended on it fled; the rest went into hiding. It's been that way ever since…until now.

"The millennium is coming."

"Wait, didn't we have one of those a few years ago?" Beth asked.

"Things are running a bit behind schedule," Michiko said with a shrug. "But this is the True Millennium. The spell cast a thousand years ago is wearing off. Magic is returning."

Beth's jaw dropped. "Seriously?"

"When's the last time you saw an ogre? In real life, not in the movies or cosplay?"

"Point…taken."

"And that's just the start. Creatures and beings that haven't been seen here in centuries are coming back. Most of them have good intentions and just want to live quiet lives, but some want to take advantage of people or exploit Earth's magical resources. And a few are set on conquest, or worse. Their goals could endanger people here and on other worlds."

"We have police and armies here," Beth said.

"Of course," Michiko said, "but when your opponents can cast spells and recruit monsters and you can't, things can get bad for you real fast, especially when the first thing every wizard learns is the spell that neutralizes gunpowder. That's where I come in."

"So you're saving the world."

"Yep!"

"On your own?" Beth said, raising an eyebrow.

"Well…I'm starting small." Michiko smiled abashedly. "But it really started with a woman named Grandmother Fox. Many years ago, she and the other members of the Council of Eight, the group she works with, saw it was time to prepare for the True Millennium. One of them told her of an orphaned baby girl destined for great things, and she took that girl in."

"And I'm guessing that girl was you."

"It was!" Michiko said. "Grandmother Fox taught me about Earth, and the stars and planets, and all the other worlds, and all the peoples and creatures you can bump into on any of them. She told me about magic, and all its good and bad uses, and she did her best to teach me right and wrong. And when I was old enough, she brought the masters in to teach me how to fight.

"At one point, one of the masters compared me to the Monkey King. I don't think he meant it as a compliment, but Grandmother Fox then joked about me being a Monkey Queen, and it stuck. Then, about a year ago, I was given my staff. They tried to tell me it was Sun Wukong's staff, but that weighed 18,000 pounds, so I doubt it. It can still do some cool things, though."

"So I noticed," Beth said. "But you're not descended from him, are you?"

"Nope. I'm no relation, and I don't have any of his mystical powers. I'm cuter than he is, though!"

"Uh-huh." Beth tried not to smile, and mostly succeeded; still, she had to admit to herself that Michiko's cheerfulness was rubbing off a little.

"But there is one thing you can do that I can't," Michiko said.

"Ummm...remember the words to 'Do You Hear The People Sing?'" Beth said.

"Besides that," Michiko said, grinning again. "Beth, you have second sight."

"Huh?"

"Let me explain. Lots of people who come here from other worlds want to blend in, at least a little. It's hard to do when you're, say, seven feet tall and purple, so they have complex illusion spells cast on themselves so they can pass for human. Those spells are called 'seemings'.

"A couple of weeks ago, I almost lost a chance to stop a faerie who wanted to cause trouble nearby. He had a very good seeming, and I couldn't tell him apart from a normal human in a crowd. I nabbed him later, though."

"So...where do I fit into this?" Beth asked.

"It's your second sight," Michiko said. "A very few humans are born able to see through and disrupt seemings and other illusions, and with practice they can look past the surface so that everyone else can see what they're hiding. That's what happened with the ogre who was after you."

"And with the Professor?"

"Who?"

"Ummm…one of my teachers?" Beth said. Michiko raised an eyebrow. "Okay, his name's Puck. You probably don't know him, though."

Michiko nodded. "I talked about this with Grandmother Fox and she said that I needed to find help, because otherwise every bad guy would try to hide behind a seeming. She cast a spell to track down someone with second sight, and that's how I found you."

The Monkey Queen smiled. "I need you, Beth. How would you like to help me save the world?"

Beth had not expected to hear that. "M-m-me?" she said.

"Yep!"

Beth stared at Michiko. She saw the scarf drifting in the evening breeze, Michiko's smile, the excitement and joy in the Monkey Queen's eyes. The geek girl part of Beth stirred, the part that wanted to chase Golden Snitches, stand with the Browncoats, ride on the Catbus, the part that wanted to take the wheel of an airship and set a course for the second star to the right. And that part almost said, *When do we start?* But the realistic side of her spoke up first.

"Michiko, I don't know," Beth said. "I'm no hero. I'm not a fighter or a wizard. I'm just a college student. Okay, maybe I'm a college student who's read every Discworld book and watches way too much *Doctor Who*, but I'm nothing special. The only things I'm good at are sewing cosplay outfits, diagramming sentences and finding plot holes in bad movies."

"Seems like you're qualified to me," Michiko said.

"But it sounds dangerous…it sounds crazy…oh, this is all too much." Beth shook her head.

"Maybe it is, but do you know something, Beth?"

"What?"

"You haven't said 'no' yet." Michiko grinned and winked.

Beth was about to reply when she realized that Michiko was right. She turned things around and around in her mind for a moment before giving up. "Can I sleep on it?" she said. "I really need more time to think it over."

"Got it. Let's get you off this roof." Michiko grabbed Beth around the waist, moved in close to her and held her staff out over the roof's edge. It stretched downward until the tip hit the ground below. Michiko, holding Beth and the staff tight, stepped off the roof.

Beth tried not to panic as the staff slowly shrunk, carrying her and Michiko down to the sidewalk. The sun had set, and the wind was blowing stronger and colder, as their feet touched the ground.

"One more thing," Michiko said as she let Beth go. "If you're still not sure I'm telling you the truth, you should talk to Puck."

"Puck?" Beth said. "You do know him?"

"Everybody knows Puck. See you soon!" And with that, Michiko sprinted down the alley and out of sight.

"Um…bye?" Beth shook her head and started down the alley, trying to take everything in. Then, she saw Puck on the far side of the quad. *What a coincidence,* a cynical part of her thought, but she still ran towards him, shouting, "Professor!"

He stopped as Beth approached him. "Lass? What are you doing out this late? Is anything wrong?"

"Oh, Professor! I just had the weirdest, craziest thing happen!"

"You found a new roommate. And she's sane."

"No! Not that! Listen…I just met a woman named Michiko who calls herself the Monkey Queen! And she rescued me from a thug who turned out to be an ogre! And she says that magic's coming back, and that she needed my help to save the world, and—" Beth stopped and took a deep breath. "And I sound like a complete lunatic right now, don't I?"

"To other people," Puck said, "yes, you would. Now, lass…this ogre you saw. He was disguised as a human?"

"Yes."

"Magically?"

"I—I think so," Beth said.

"And you disrupted his disguise?"

"Yes."

Puck nodded. "And when we were talking earlier…did you notice something different about me?" Beth blushed and looked down, too embarrassed to speak.

"Beth." She looked up again, almost in shock; she couldn't remember the last time Puck had called her by her name. "Michiko had told me she was looking for help. I had no idea it would turn out to be you, and I'm both worried sick and overjoyed that it is.

"It could be dangerous, make no mistake about that. But it will also be the greatest adventure you could ever hope to have. You will see sights no one else from this world has ever seen, go places you never thought you'd go. And you'll have friends, allies stout and true."

Puck laid a hand on Beth's shoulder. "Whatever you decide, lass, remember what I said earlier about change. Your life is in for quite a bit of it."

Beth nodded, almost dizzy from everything Puck and Michiko had told her. "I should get home," she managed to say.

"Of course. It's late. But one more thing, lass."

"And that is?"

"Do try not to wreck my seeming here on campus. I have enough trouble with the dean as it is. Good night." Puck turned and walked away.

"Night," Beth said. She hurried off, hoping the burrito place was still open.

It was, and the to-go order with an overstuffed burrito and a bag of freshly-made tortilla chips helped clear Beth's head. She walked briskly down the street, heading for her apartment. She wasn't sure what Saturday might bring, but at least she had her dinner, and no matter how weird things were getting, they could be put off just a little longer. The front door to her building opened as it always did due to the lock being broken, the mail was waiting, and nothing out of the ordinary lurked on the three creaky flights of stairs that led up to her apartment.

That part came when Beth got to her apartment door. Michiko was sitting on the welcome mat, calmly sipping on a smoothie, a bag of chips nearby. "Um…hi?" Michiko said with a smile.

Beth sighed. "You know," she said, "I should be surprised, but I'm not."

"Chips?" Michiko held up her bag.

"Got some already. How…how did you find me?"

"We should talk inside," Michiko said as she stood up. Beth nodded, slipped past her, and unlocked the apartment door.

As roommates had come and gone, Beth had moved more of her stuff into the small living room, to the point where her next roommate would have to squeeze any plants and decor she had in with the bookshelves, posters and DVD racks. It was cluttered and crowded, especially with the huge couch taking up the middle of the room, but it was clean and cozy. "I like your place!" Michiko said as Beth locked the door behind them. "Hardwood floors!"

"It's nice," Beth said. "So…"

"Oh, right." Michiko turned to face Beth. "It's the spell that Grandmother Fox cast. She didn't find out everything about you, but she did find your address and that you were going to Cooper."

"She doesn't work for the NSA, does she?"

Michiko giggled. "I hope not!"

"So why are you here?" Beth asked.

"If Grandmother Fox found you," the Monkey Queen said, "so could others. Like that ogre did." Her tone was suddenly serious, and Beth had to hold back a shudder. "I want to be sure you're safe. If I'm making you uncomfortable, I'll wait outside."

Beth didn't have to think it over. She was worried about unwelcome visitors, and she also had to admit to herself that she was reassured, and even a little bit glad, to see Michiko. "Okay," she said. "You can stay here tonight, but no loud noises and no company."

"Okay!" Michiko said, the seriousness gone again.

"If you get cold, there's a spare blanket in the closet in the empty bedroom. There's a bathroom next to the kitchen." Beth pointed towards one side of the living room, across from the bedrooms. "If you get bored, the TV remote is on the table by the couch. Remember, not too loud."

"What about you?"

"I've had a long day," Beth said. "I just want to go into my bedroom, eat my burrito, and go to bed. We'll talk tomorrow morning."

"Okay. Good night!" Michiko said with a smile.

"Night." Beth went into her bedroom and closed the door. She thought about locking it, but she then realized it probably wouldn't do any good anyway.

Beth downed her burrito, her chips, a can of diet soda she kept in the tiny fridge in her small bedroom, and a dark chocolate bar from her secret stash for good measure. She checked her e-mail, her Facebook page, and a dozen other websites. Finally, her thoughts started to drift away from everything she had seen and heard during her long day. Michiko was keeping quiet, thankfully, and Beth changed into her pajamas and got ready for bed.

Then she heard the scratching at her living room window. A chill crept down her spine as she quietly opened the bedroom door and peeked out.

MythBusters was on, but Michiko wasn't watching. She was standing at the window, staff in hand. Outside the window, Beth could see the outline of a large black bird, possibly a crow. It glared at Michiko, and something sinister and shadowy lurked in its glowing red eyes.

The Monkey Queen spoke. "Go. Tell whoever commands you. Tell the world. Beth is under my protection. You will not have her, you will not harm her. Go."

The bird cawed and flew off, darkness trailing in its wake. Michiko sat back down on the couch. Beth softly closed the bedroom door and dropped into bed, staring at the ceiling. Sleep took a long time to come as one thought played over and over in her mind—*What in the world have I gotten myself into?*

Chapter Three

Beth opened her eyes, rolled over in bed, and squinted at her alarm clock. She scowled sleepily. It was Saturday, and she'd earned the right to sleep in. She snuggled back under the covers.

Then, Beth sat up as she remembered she had company. She gave up on going back to sleep and reached for her glasses with a sigh. She got out of bed, wrapped an old black and white plaid bathrobe over her blue flannel pajamas, and stuck her feet into a pair of pink bunny slippers. She opened the bedroom door and cautiously poked her head out.

"Good morning!" Michiko shouted from the small kitchen.

"Morning," Beth mumbled as she shuffled into the living room.

"Cute slippers!"

"Hey, I like these slippers—" Beth stopped. Her nose twitched. "You…you made coffee. You made coffee! Thankyouthankyouthankyou!"

Michiko smiled as Beth dashed into the kitchen, grabbed a mug and fixed her coffee. She took her first sip, and was about to have a second when a thought made her pause. "You've already had some, haven't you?" Beth asked.

"Two cups!" Michiko said cheerfully.

"We're doomed." Beth took a longer sip. "Oh, by the way, all I have for breakfast is stale oatmeal and your leftover chips. And bread, but I'm out of jam."

"That's okay," Michiko said. "Sooo…"

"Your offer."

"Yeah."

"Well…" Beth took another sip of her coffee and stared down into the cup. She still hadn't decided. She had no idea what the right decision was. "Michiko…I…"

There was a knock at the door. Beth glanced up. "Were you expecting anyone?" she said softly to Michiko.

"Nope. You?"

"No."

Michiko nodded, crept to the door and glanced through the peephole. "Did you know the men in black are after us?" she asked as they knocked again, harder. "You need to get that front door fixed."

The apartment shook slightly from the third knock. "Let them in," Beth said with a sigh. "I'll probably get a noise complaint if we don't."

Michiko sprung to the couch, grabbed her staff, jumped back to the door and swung it open. "Good morning!" she said as three men pushed past her into the apartment.

As one of them shut the door, Beth understood why Michiko had made the "men in black" reference. They were all dressed in matching black suits and ties, and they all wore identical sunglasses. They all stood stiffly straight, and they all scowled as they glanced around the living room. "Where is he?" one of them said.

"He?" Beth asked.

"Beth, are you hiding something?" Michiko said.

"Monkey Queen—" the man said.

"She's just full of surprises."

"Enough!" the man in black shouted. "We want answers, Monkey Queen."

Michiko grinned and leaned against the back of the couch. "I don't even know what the questions are. Do you, Beth?"

"I think someone here is hiding something," Beth said, kicking herself mentally for not getting the hint earlier. She took a breath, reminded herself of what Michiko had said about looking below the surface, stared at the men and blinked.

The air around the three men wavered for a moment. Then, their seemings vanished.

The men were actually tall, blond and slender, wearing elegant red tunics with gold trim over what appeared to be chainmail. Emblazoned on their tunics was the image of a diamond, bordered with gold. All three had swords, sheathed but close at hand. Their eyes were a deep green, and their ears came to perfect points. They glared at Beth, who barely concealed her surprise.

"So, you're from Duke Wrexham's court," Michiko said.

"I am Cantwick," one of the men said. "We want to know the whereabouts of Puck."

"He left the Courts of Faerie long ago. Why is he so important to you now?"

Cantwick folded his arms. "Because he was abducted late last night."

Beth gasped. Michiko's eyes narrowed. "How do you know this?" she asked.

"Our liege Wrexham was to meet with him last night," the faerie said. "When he didn't show up, we searched for him. We found signs of a struggle on a side street nearby."

"So why are you bothering us?"

"You and your oddly-dressed friend were the last ones to see him that we know of."

"Hey!" Beth said.

Michiko sighed. "We're both friends of his. Why would we want to kidnap him?"

"You humans are bizarre, irrational creatures," Cantwick said with a sneer. "What other race would wear such ridiculous clothing?"

"I like these bunny slippers," Beth said.

"Well, we didn't do it," Michiko said. "He's not here."

"In that case," Cantwick said, "there will be no objection to us searching this place?"

"You're darned right there's—" Beth started to say. Michiko grabbed her arm and shushed her as the faeries started their search. They were quick but efficient, and though they checked every nook and cranny, they refrained from digging into Beth's belongings any more than necessary. All the while, Beth fumed.

After the search, the faeries held a quick conference in the living room, then turned towards the women. "So Puck is not here," Cantwick said.

"Told you," Michiko said. "Did you have fun poking around her underwear drawer?"

"I tire of you, Earthling," the faerie said. "And your lunatic friend."

Something inside Beth snapped. She stormed up to Cantwick. "And I have had it with you and your attitude!" she shouted, jabbing a finger into his sternum. "And this oddly dressed human lunatic wants you out of her apartment now!" Out of the corner of her eye, she could see Michiko grinning.

The faerie smiled unpleasantly. "Perhaps you should come with us," he said. "Our liege may be interested in you and your second sight." He lifted a hand; Beth quickly stepped back.

Michiko snapped her staff in front of Cantwick, blocking his way. "I'm pretty sure you're not her type," she said.

Cantwick lowered his hand with a scowl. He turned and opened the door; his companions followed him out as their seemings reappeared. "We'll be watching both of you," he said as Beth shut and locked the door behind him.

"There's a disgusting thought," Beth said with a smile. "So, Michiko, do you really—"

Michiko had pulled a smartphone from her pocket, and was holding it by her ear; she held up her free hand, and Beth stopped mid-sentence. She stood in silence for a minute. "I just called Puck," she said as she hung up. "No answer, but I missed a call while I was in the shower."

"When did you take a shower?"

"While the coffee was brewing. Let me check my voicemail."

Michiko dialed another number. As she listened, her eyes narrowed. "Beth," she said, "you should hear this. I'll put it on speaker." Beth nodded and moved closer.

"Hello? Monkey Queen?" the voice in the message said. "My name is Tierra. I'm a friend of Puck's. Something happened last night. I think he's been kidnapped. I didn't know who to call until I remembered he gave me your number in case of an emergency. And I'm worried that the kidnappers may have seen me. Please, Monkey Queen, help me."

Michiko turned the speaker off and put her phone away. "So the faeries weren't lying?" Beth said.

"No. And I don't know what kind of danger he's in." Beth could hear the concern in Michiko's voice. "Puck's my friend too. I need to talk to Tierra. I need to find him." She reached for her staff.

"Don't you mean, we need to find him?" Beth found herself saying.

"Huh?" Michiko turned back to Beth.

"Michiko…" Beth swallowed. "I'm still not sure I can handle any of this. I'm not ready. I don't know if I ever will be. But if a friend of mine is in trouble, I'm not going to sit around and do nothing. I'm going to help."

"Does that mean…?"

Beth nodded. "I'm in. I don't know if I can help you save the world, but I'll help you find Puck. After that, we'll see."

"Partners, then?" Michiko grinned and held out her hand.

"Partners." Beth shook hands with Michiko and smiled.

"Yaaay!" Michiko pulled Beth close and gave her a big hug; she was too startled to react. "We need breakfast, and we'll have to eat on the way," Michiko said as she let go of Beth. "I'll grab something while you're in the shower. Muffins okay?"

"They'll be fine," Beth said. "But don't you need to change?"

"This first." Michiko lifted her staff, and it quickly shrunk to the size of a small flashlight; she slipped it into her pocket. Then, she whistled, and suddenly her clothes changed; she was wearing a baggy yellow sweater and black jeans. "Don't blink and ruin my seeming!" she said with a grin.

"I'll try not to," Beth said as Michiko opened the apartment door.

"And you need to wear shoes!" Michiko said as she left. "No bunny slippers!"

"Oh, you're just jealous!" Beth shouted as she closed the door. She could still hear the Monkey Queen's laughter, and she couldn't help but smile.

Chapter Four

It was a nice Saturday morning, not too foggy or warm, and the streets were uncrowded as Michiko and Beth walked along, munching on blueberry bran muffins. "These are yummy!" Michiko said.

"Yeah. That coffeehouse always has good ones. Fresh, too." Beth sipped her coffee. "Did you know the Professor is allergic to blueberries?"

"Really?"

"Yeah. Last semester, I went through a baking phase. I made a batch of blueberry muffins, and I gave him one. He took one bite and swelled up like he was stung by a bee. I'm surprised he's still talking to me."

"Are you sure it wasn't just your baking?" Michiko said. Beth blew a raspberry at her, and she laughed.

"So, why were those faeries so concerned that Puck was kidnapped?" Beth asked. "He's just a college professor."

"He is now," Michiko said, "but he used to be kind of a big deal back in Faerie."

"How big?"

"He was a royal advisor to half a dozen Dukes at one time or another."

Beth whistled. "I had no idea."

"He doesn't like to talk about it much." Michiko took a long drink of coffee and added, "Puck kept moving from court to court. He really wanted to try to make things better for everyone in Faerie, but none of the Dukes would listen."

"That's why he came here?"

"Part of it. There were also rumors surrounding his departure. Wrexham may have planted some of them."

"Got it." Beth finished her muffin. "Hey, how much further do we have to go?"

"Not too much." They were out of the town center now, heading up a hill towards the woods that surrounded the town on three sides. The redwood trees were sparse on the outskirts, but they were more numerous and taller the further out one went from town. "Puck told me that Tierra had a small cottage out here," Michiko said.

"Did you try calling her back?"

"I did, while I was getting breakfast. She didn't pick up." Michiko paused, then added, "I don't blame her. She sounded scared."

Beth was quiet for a minute as she finished her coffee. Then, she looked down an unpaved trail set well off the road. She could see a small white cottage surrounded by a low picket fence near the trail, mostly concealed by trees and bushes. "Do you think that's it?" she asked.

Michiko nodded and put a finger to her lips. "The front door's open," she whispered; she snapped her fingers, and her seeming vanished. "Follow my lead." Beth nodded back.

They moved quietly down the trail until they reached the cottage. Michiko carefully stepped up to the open door and peered inside. "I don't see anyone—" she started to say.

"Michiko!" Beth shouted. "Over here!"

The Monkey Queen turned and saw three young men coming around the side of the house. They were wearing jeans, black vests over t-shirts, and bandanas, reminding Beth of extras from 1980s gang movies. One of them was dragging a petite woman who wore a long flowery dress. His hand was covering her mouth, but it slipped, and the woman shouted, "Help! Help me!"

Michiko pulled her miniaturized staff from her pocket; in half a second, it had grown back to its normal size. Beth stared at the thugs, reminded herself to look past the surface, and blinked.

The seemings wavered, then vanished. They were disguising a trio who were neither human or faerie. They were shorter than humans, with red scaly skin, spiky black hair and taloned fingers. Their ears were big, their eyes were wide and black with red pupils, and their mouths were filled with sharp teeth. They wore black robes with swordbelts, holding blades with thick, black hilts, buckled in place. The woman they were abducting was a faerie, gray-haired and dark-skinned, with the same pointed ears as Wrexham's men. "Goblins?" Beth said; the trio seemed to be fuzzy, like they were out of focus.

"Hobgoblins," Michiko said as they noticed her. "Okay, boys," she said to them, "trick or treat is so over. Let the lady go, or no candy for you."

"Monkey Queen!" one of the hobgoblins said, pointing at her. "This is none of your business. Back away."

Michiko twirled her staff. "Or what?"

The hobgoblin reached for his sword. Before he could pull it from its sheath, Michiko had covered the twenty feet between them and struck his arm with her staff. As he yelped with pain, she spun around and hit another hobgoblin in his stomach; he crumpled over, gasping for breath.

Michiko stared angrily at the last hobgoblin, who was still holding the faerie. "It's no fun when they fight back, is it?" she said. "Go ahead. Try something. You'll be sorry."

The hobgoblin threw the faerie to the ground and ran off, his comrades scurrying after him. Michiko ignored them as she knelt by the woman. "Are you all right, ma'am?" she asked.

She nodded. "Thank you," she said.

"You're welcome. You're Tierra, right?"

"I am. And you must be the Monkey Queen."

"My friends call me Michiko." She grinned. "That's my partner, Beth McGill." Beth smiled and waved. "Need a hand?"

"Yes, please." The faerie took Michiko's hand and got to her feet.

"Beth?" Michiko asked. "Did you see where the hobgoblins went?"

"I saw them going back down the trail," Beth said. "They stayed clear of the house."

"Let's go in, then," Michiko said. "I have an idea about who, but I'm still hoping I'm wrong."

Tierra's cottage was sparsely furnished, but there were chairs for all three of them, and reheated herbal tea helped to restore the faerie's strength. "I can't thank you enough, Michiko," she said. "Those hobgoblins, they just burst in and grabbed me!"

"I know." Michiko patted Tierra's hand. "But how did you wind up all the way out here?"

"Well…" The faerie stopped and looked at Beth.

"You can trust her," Michiko said. "I do." Beth smiled.

Tierra nodded. "I haven't been here long," she said. "I just came here a month, month and a half ago. I was tired of all the arguing and fighting back home. I just wanted peace, and to get back to nature.

"I had heard that Puck could help me get settled in, so I went to see him. He was so nice, so helpful. He found this little place for me; I was worried that it was a bit out of the way, but he was sure it would be fine.

"I was supposed to meet him in town last night; I wanted to treat him to dinner to thank him to all he had done for me. We were going to that Thai place, down on Leiber Lane."

"Not Wonderland?" Michiko asked. Beth raised an eyebrow, but kept quiet.

"I really wanted to try Thai food," Tierra said. "Puck was happy with that."

"He would be," Beth said. "He loves spicy food."

"What happened when you got to the restaurant?" Michiko asked.

Tierra shifted in her chair. "I got there a bit early, so I waited outside. After about half an hour, I was starting to get worried, so I took a quick walk around the block to see if I could find him. As I did, I glanced down an alley. That's where I saw them."

"Them?"

"It was a group of four people. I wasn't sure what was going on at first, but then I saw Puck. He hadn't seen me, but it looked like he was trying to get away, and the other three were holding him back. One of them saw me, and he looked so angry! I turned away and ran.

"I went straight home, and tried to call Puck again and again, but he didn't answer. I finally called you, and I thought it was you when those men came by, because we don't get a lot of humans up here."

"Tierra…" Michiko looked into the faerie's eyes. "Those hobgoblins who were trying to abduct you? Were they the same ones you saw with Puck last night?"

After a long moment, Tierra nodded. "I'm scared," she said. Her hands shook. "I'm scared that they'll come back for me."

"We need to get you somewhere safe," Michiko said. "Beth and I will need to leave soon. When we do, we'll make sure the hobgoblins are gone. Then, I'll call a friend, an Emigre named Windsor. He'll get you to a safe house for a few days."

"How will I know it's him?"

"I'll tell him to say 'Michiko and Beth sent me' when he gets here, and not to mention 'Monkey Queen' like the hobgoblins would."

"I could stay with her," Beth said.

Michiko shook her head. "We don't have any time to waste," she said. "I'll need your help to look for clues." She turned back to Tierra. "Lock your doors when we leave. Call me if anyone who isn't Windsor tries to get in."

"I will." Tierra swallowed. "Please, Michiko, find Puck."

"We will. Count on it." Michiko smiled.

Michiko and Beth failed to turn up any sign of the hobgoblins in a quick search around Tierra's cottage, to their relief. As they finished the search, Michiko made a quick phone call. Beth wasn't close enough to hear it clearly, which only whetted her curiosity.

"All done!" Michiko said as she hung up. "Let's get back to town."

"Where to?" Beth asked as they started back down the trail.

"That Thai restaurant. We need to start looking for clues."

"Didn't Tierra confirm that the people who attacked her were the ones who she saw with Puck?" Beth said.

"She did, but we need proof if we're going to confront the hobgoblins."

"Okay. So, what are hobgoblins doing here? On Earth?"

"They're Emigres," Michiko said. "Like Puck."

"He's not a hobgoblin."

"No, but they both come from the same place, and for the same reason—to get away from Faerie.

"It all goes back to the coming of the True Millennium. Before magic was closed off, there were several interdimensional portals between Earth and Faerie, and even a few between Earth and other worlds. They're known as 'auldgates'. The closing of magic caused all those auldgates to close as well, but now that magic is returning, they're starting to reopen. The first was one that opened about thirty years ago."

"And where was that one?" Beth asked.

"Oh, about half a mile or so back up this trail." Michiko grinned.

"That's when Puck started teaching at Cooper!" Beth said. "Does that mean what I think it means?"

"Yep! He wasn't the first through when the auldgate reopened, but he was the first to stay. He told me once that he had heard about Earth for decades, and he decided that this was a good place to go when he left Faerie for good. Word got around and since then, even though the Courts have tried to stop it, there's been a trickle of people migrating here ever since. They call themselves 'Emigres'."

"It's not just faeries, is it?" Beth asked as they approached the town. "Hey, don't forget your seeming."

Michiko nodded and whistled softly, and she was again wearing her sweater and jeans. "No, it's not. There's a pixie and gremlin settlement, a dwarven community, and a few brownies. And others."

"Including hobgoblins."

"There's a smallish group here. They tend to keep to themselves."

"So what's so bad about Faerie?" Beth asked. "Why would they want to leave?"

"Well," Michiko said, "Faerie is split between the Courts, which is where the faeries live, and the Outlands, where everyone else lives. The Dukes at Court usually split their time between intrigue, infighting and harassing the Outlands, with the occasional war to break up the tedium. A fair number of people there get fed up with everything and sneak over here, and some come here after getting in trouble or being exiled. Some of them try to blend in with human society, some stay in their own communities, and some try to live on their own."

"And Windsor? And Wonderland?"

"Tell you about both later. We're here." They had reached Leiber Lane and the Thai restaurant. "There should be an alley nearby."

"Several, actually," Beth said, "and not all of them pretty and well-lit. It's not the nicest part of town."

"Got it," Michiko said as they headed down a side street. "And I see what you mean." She pointed at the entrance to a narrow alley up the street. Yellow "caution" tape had been put up across the entrance, and three policemen were standing in front of it.

Beth grabbed Michiko's arm and pulled her back. "Don't tell me you're on their most wanted list!" Michiko said with a grin.

"Not yet, I hope," Beth said, "but there's something wrong here."

"How so?"

"Their uniforms. They're not what the police here in town wear."

"You're right." Michiko's eyes narrowed. "Move back down the street. When I drop my seeming, see what you can see." Beth nodded and backed away slowly, keeping an eye on Michiko as she walked up to the policemen.

"Good morning!" Michiko said. "What's going on, officer?"

"Police business," one of them told her.

"Oooh!" Michiko said. "What happened?"

"Confidential," the policeman said. "Move along now."

"What? You ran out of donuts and now you're all cranky?"

The policeman loomed angrily over Michiko. "Are you trying to be funny?"

"I don't have to try," she said. She snapped her fingers, and her seeming vanished.

Beth jumped on her cue, tried to look past the surface, and blinked. The other seemings disappeared, and where there had been police, there were now hobgoblins, a different trio than at Tierra's cottage, armored and drawing swords. Again, Beth noticed that they seemed fuzzy; she hoped nothing was wrong with her eyes or her head.'

Michiko sprung back, reached into her pocket and pulled out her mini-sized staff; it quickly grew to its normal size. "Yay!" she said. "I haven't beaten anyone up in the last twenty minutes!"

The lead hobgoblin advanced on Michiko, sword held out. She held her staff in both hands, watching out for the others as she circled around, looking for an opening. She saw a quick gleam of light in the corner of her eye. She spun around and hit the biggest hobgoblin in the hand with her staff; he grimaced and dropped his sword.

Michiko spun back just in time as the other hobgoblins swung their swords at her. She parried their blows, then swung her staff; they jumped back, out of its way. She took two steps back.

The hobgoblin who Michiko had disarmed grabbed her elbows, pinning her arms behind her back. "Where are your taunts now, Monkey Queen!" he said. Beth gasped as the other hobgoblins advanced on Michiko, swords raised, smiling cruelly.

Michiko braced herself against the hobgoblin behind her and quickly brought her knees up to her chest. She then kicked out hard, catching the advancing hobgoblins in their sternums and knocking them over. She planted her feet and snapped her head back, hitting the hobgoblin who was restraining her in the face. He yelped in pain and released her, clutching his right eye.

The other hobgoblins were getting up. Michiko grabbed the one who had held her, spun him around, and pushed him into the others; they fell into a tangled heap. "Had enough?" Michiko said with a grin, twirling her staff. "Or shall I taunt you some more?"

The hobgoblins got up, grabbed their swords and backed away. "Next time, Monkey Queen!" their leader said as they hurried off.

"I'll mark my calendar!" she shouted after them.

"Wow," Beth said as she walked up to Michiko. "That—that was…"

"That was fun!" Michiko said with a wide smile.

"Yeah, that's one way of putting it. I guess."

"Now, let's see what they were trying to cover up here." Michiko headed for the alley.

Beth started after her, getting her first look down the alley. It seemed to be empty, except for piles of trash, empty cardboard boxes and overturned garbage cans. Then, she sensed more than saw something in the narrow entrance. She blinked; then, she grabbed and tugged at Michiko's arm. "Wait! Michiko, wait!" she said.

Michiko stopped. "You should have gone before we left," she said.

"No! There's something wrong!" Beth pointed at the alley.

"What?"

"Well…it's a bit hard to describe, but there's something blocking the entrance to the alley. I looked at it, and there seemed to be…ripples in the air, like a curtain in the breeze."

"Really!" Michiko said. "Let's test it." She backed away from the entrance, followed by Beth. Then, she took a penny from her pocket, leaned forward, and lobbed it towards the alley. When it reached the entrance, it suddenly rebounded back at Michiko and Beth, shooting past them and leaving a dent in the mailbox across the street.

They moved further away from the alley. "What was that?" Beth said. "A magic wall of some sort?"

"Yep. And if I'd tried to go in there, it wouldn't have gone well." Michiko grinned. "Your second sight just kept me from getting hurt. Thanks!"

"Don't mention it," Beth said; she tried to sound casual, but she knew she was blushing. "So what now?"

"It's obvious that someone wanted that alley left alone. We need to get in there."

"Could I disrupt that wall?"

Michiko shook her head. "Second sight isn't much good against barrier spells. We're going to need help."

"But who?" Beth asked. "Where?"

"Come on. I have an idea."

Chapter Five

After a brisk walk, Michiko and Beth reached a cul-de-sac at the top of a hill and stopped in front of a three-story Victorian house that looked older than the queen that style of architecture had been named after. For all its age, though, it looked very well kept and inviting, with paint that looked relatively new and plant-filled windowboxes.

"Your turn to see my place!" Michiko said as she stood at the front door and pulled a set of keys from her pocket. Beth waited two steps behind her, not sure what to expect.

Then, the door opened. At first, Beth thought there was no one there. Then, she looked down past Michiko and saw a very short, wrinkled man. He had pale skin, a long beard and plain clothing. "Mistress Michiko," he said, bowing politely. "Good morning."

"Hi, Feng!" Michiko said. "Is the big boss up yet?"

"She's upstairs," Feng said as Michiko entered the house; Beth followed them cautiously into the large, bright foyer. "I suspect she was expecting both of you."

"She's like that," Michiko said. "Feng, this is Beth McGill, my partner."

"For now," Beth said, glancing along the walls at the art hanging there, Chinese watercolors and Japanese prints.

"For now," Feng said. "If you would?" He gestured towards a stairway near the front door.

Michiko and Beth followed Feng up the two well-worn flights of stairs. At the top was a short hallway with a single door at the end. Feng opened the door and stood to one side as Michiko and Beth walked in. "Wow," Beth said, her eyes widening.

Behind the doorway was an indoor garden. It seemed that it was larger than the house that held it. There were dwarf trees, flowering bushes, cobblestone paths, grassy swaths. In the distance, Beth could swear that she heard a waterfall.

There was a small stone bench near the door. Sitting on it was a woman in a plain, flowing, full-length white dress with gold stitching and billowing sleeves. She was tall and regal. Her hair was long and black and her skin was smooth, but her eyes seemed to shine with years of wisdom tinged with kindness.

She rose and turned to face the two women. "Michiko," she said in a soft, clear voice. "You brought company."

"Yeah," Michiko said with an embarrassed grin. "Her name's Beth McGill. Beth, this is Grandmother Fox."

"I am honored." Grandmother Fox bowed to Beth, who returned the bow. "Is she the one I told you about?" she asked Michiko.

The Monkey Queen nodded. "She's my partner."

"For now," Beth said. "She needs my help."

"There is a problem?" Grandmother Fox asked.

"It's Puck. He's been kidnapped."

Grandmother Fox listened with a grim expression as Beth and Michiko told their story. When they finished, she stared into the distance for a minute. "So, you cannot search the alley," she said.

Michiko nodded. "If someone went through that kind of trouble to put up a barrier spell, they may be afraid that we'll find something."

Grandmother Fox gestured and Feng, who had been waiting by the door, ran over. She leaned down and whispered in his ear; he hurried out of the garden. "Michiko," she said, "this may take a while. Why don't you show Beth around?"

"Okay!" Michiko set off down a cobblestone path, Beth following.

"So what do you think?" Michiko asked after they had walked along the path for a minute. A light breeze blew a leaf alongside them.

"It's beautiful!" Beth said. "But I'm still wondering how this all fits into the top floor of an old Victorian." A butterfly fluttered by.

"I asked Grandmother Fox that once, when I was younger. She said that someday, after I had learned much and traveled far, I might begin to grasp the basic concepts."

"Oh. I thought it might be tesseracts."

"Me too." Michiko grinned. "I didn't want to spook her, though."

"But you live here!" Beth said. "You grew up here! That's so cool!"

"Yep! I used to play here all the time after tutoring and practice. Now, I just come up here to stretch after my morning workout, and when I need some quiet time."

"Which is when?"

"Not that often."

"No surprise there." Beth smiled. "You know, when I was a kid, I would have loved to have had a secret place. I used to hide under the covers late at night with a flashlight, reading about places like this when I should have been sleeping. This would have been like heaven."

"But you know the trouble with secret places?" Michiko asked.

"You can't stay there forever?" Beth said.

"Right! Grandmother Fox taught me that. You can't hide from the world, and it's more fun not to."

"She has a point."

"She's very wise. Speaking of..." Michiko pointed towards Grandmother Fox, standing by her stone bench.

Beth's jaw dropped. "How? We were just walking away from her, straight down the path!"

"When Grandmother Fox wants to see you, the path leads to her. And no, I have no idea how that works."

They saw that Grandmother Fox was holding something in one hand as they approached her. It was a small jade carving in the shape of a fox, suspended from a leather strap. She gave it to Michiko while saying, "When you leave here, this will guide you to where you need to go."

"And who will we find there?" Michiko asked.

"I have heard tell," Grandmother Fox said, "of a sorcerer who may be of some assistance to our cause. He once was powerful, but has seen his standing and stature reduced of late. I hope he can be persuaded to help." Michiko nodded and hung the pendant around her neck.

As she did, Beth said, "Grandmother Fox? This place..." She took another look around the garden. "It's beautiful. Thank you for letting me visit."

"You're welcome." Grandmother Fox smiled. "I'm glad to see that you're getting along with Michiko. I want you to know that no matter which path you choose to take, this house is your safe haven. You will always be welcome here."

"Thank you." Beth smiled back gratefully.

"As for you, Michiko..."

"Is this the part where you give me the usual sage advice?" Michiko said.

"Hmph. Just two words this time: Be careful." Grandmother Fox bent down and kissed Michiko on the cheek. She reddened and squirmed, but Beth could tell she was trying to hide a smile.

As soon as Michiko and Beth had left the house and reached the sidewalk, the Monkey Queen stopped and touched the fox pendant. "This way," she said. She whistled softly to reset her seeming and headed off down the hill, back to the center of town, Beth following.

After a few minutes, Michiko stopped and pointed across the street. "That's where we need to go," she said.

"A...pet store?" Beth scowled.

Michiko shrugged. "It's where the pendant led me." She closed her eyes and pressed her hand against her sternum; Beth guessed that she was checking the information that Grandmother Fox's spell had stored inside the pendant.

"Still there?" Beth asked as Michiko opened her eyes.

"He or she seems to be staying put." Michiko grinned. "That gives us time for lunch!"

"Oh, dear, wherever shall we find a place to eat?" Beth said in a deadpan voice, pointing at the sandwich shop next to the pet store. Michiko giggled.

They ate their lunches quickly and without much conversation; Michiko kept checking her pendant to make sure the one they were searching for hadn't moved. As they left the sandwich shop, Beth said, "You know, Michiko, I had a question."

"Is it about whether that place delivers?" Michiko asked. "Their tomato soup was yummy!"

"Not that. Why did it take so long for me to see through Puck's seeming? I've known him for months."

"Good question." Michiko thought for a moment. "Puck's probably used that seeming for years," she said. "The older the seeming, the harder it is to see through it."

Beth nodded. "So why did my second sight kick in when it did?"

"Have you been under a lot of stress lately?" Michiko asked. "That's been known to trigger things like second sight."

"Friday was pretty rough," Beth said.

"There you go!" Michiko smiled as they stepped inside the pet store. It was good-sized and somewhat crowded; pet lovers picking up supplies mingled with families with hopeful children. Michiko wound her way through the shoppers and shelves; Beth kept up as best as she could.

In the back of the store were the pet cages. A sign referred those looking for cats and dogs to the nearby shelter, but there were still plenty of birds and hamsters. Michiko glanced at them, but turned away when she saw the guinea pigs.

They were in a freestanding plastic display, divided into smaller enclosures. The guinea pigs there were eating or grooming or sniffing around, except for one small black and white pig who was sleeping in a corner. "Oooh!" Michiko squealed. "They're so cuuute!"

"Um, Michiko," Beth said, "are you sure this is the best—"

"Excuse me," Michiko said to a passing store employee. "Could you tell me more about these guinea pigs?"

"Well," the employee said, "we just got them in a few weeks ago. They've all had checkups, and they've been spayed or neutered."

"Could I see that black and white one in the corner?"

"You should use the hand sanitizer first." Michiko did so as the employee opened the cage and carefully lifted the animal out. "This one's a young bull pig. He's a bit of an odd one, though."

"Odd?" Beth asked as Michiko took the guinea pig; his eyes opened, and he looked around frantically.

"Well, guinea pigs are usually very social animals, but this one tends to keep to himself."

"And?"

The employee sighed. "He seems to like watching the store TV."

Michiko stroked the guinea pig, who tried to wriggle out of her hands. "He's so cute!" she chirped. "We'll take him."

"What?" Beth said.

"Excellent choice," said the employee. "Now, you'll need food, and a cage, and bedding…"

The pet store wasn't too far from Beth's apartment, so Michiko led the way there, carrying all the supplies. Beth trailed behind with the guinea pig, who was curled up in the corner of his cage, and a sullen expression.

As soon as they were in the apartment, Beth set the cage on a table by the couch and turned to face Michiko. "What do you think you're doing?" she said.

Michiko blinked. "Huh?"

"We're supposed to be finding help to rescue Puck, and you drop everything to buy a pet!" Beth pointed at the guinea pig, who glared at her.

"But—"

"Am I going to have to feed it?" Beth asked. "And clean its cage?"

"I'll help," Michiko said meekly.

The guinea pig wheeped. "I wasn't talking to you!" Beth shouted. "You didn't want to come with us anyway!"

"Now, Gregor," Michiko said, "be nice."

Beth raised an eyebrow. "Who names a guinea pig 'Gregor'?"

"My parents did, you fool!" the guinea pig said in a raspy voice.

Beth jumped back from the table. "He...talks?" she said.

"Very observant, this one."

"Now that he finally got his vocal spell in place, he can," Michiko said.

"Vocal spell—wait." Beth's eyes widened. "He's the one that Grandmother Fox sent us to find? The sorcerer who's supposed to help us?"

"Yep."

"Oh." Beth blushed. "I should have known. I'm sorry I yelled at you, Michiko."

"That's okay. Gregor, why don't you tell us about yourself?" Michiko said with a smile.

The guinea pig sighed. "My name is Gregor, and I am wishing I was back at the pet store instead of talking to this crazy woman. How's that?"

"Vague and insulting," Beth said.

"Perfect." Gregor turned away. "I didn't want this, you know. A thousand years ago, I was a mighty sorcerer! I was feared by everyone! The Terror of the Western Steppes!"

"He really wasn't that terrible," Michiko said to Beth. "He just liked to brag."

"So what happened?" Beth asked.

"He refused to help defend Earth with the Monkey King and the others," Michiko said. "He got greedy instead, tried to build his fortune."

"And?"

"He was stampeded by a herd of yaks."

"Ouch." Beth winced.

"And then," Gregor said, "my soul wandered for a thousand years, until I was told I had a chance to atone. I agreed to reincarnation." He gestured angrily with his little forepaws. "They didn't tell me about this part of the deal!"

"Well, you know what they say about karma," Beth said.

Gregor ignored her. "I used to be fear incarnate. Now...I'm small and furry."

"And cute!" Michiko said. She reached into the cage and stroked Gregor's head. "What a little cutie-wutie you are! Yes you are!"

"Kill me now."

"So," Beth said in a voice that was a little too cheerful, "shall we let Gregor know about what's going on?"

Gregor's eyes gleamed. "How about I tell you about the Monkey King instead?"

"Oh, we can save that for later—"

"After this fool gets herself killed? I knew Sun Wukong, and this idiot couldn't hold a candle to him! 'Monkey Queen'. Ha!" Gregor snorted.

Michiko's expression darkened. "Now, there's no—" Beth started to say.

"Not that he was any brain trust either," Gregor said. "Full of hot air, always boasting—hey, Blondie! Would you like to hear a joke?"

"Not really," Beth said.

"Do you know why monkeys are brown?"

"I—"

"Because the Monkey King kissed Buddha's butt!" Gregor shouted. "Buddha licked him good, and the Monkey King said, 'Oh merciful Buddha, my lips do not deserve to—'"

Gregor stopped talking and winced as Michiko whacked his cage with her open hand. "Stop being so mean!" she yelled.

"Well, stop being so belittling and condescending to me!" Gregor said. "Like it or not, and I don't, I'm on your side! Show me some respect!"

"But I was just having fun!" Michiko said. "I didn't—"

"Michiko," Beth said. "Let it go."

"But—"

"I mean it. We have to work together with Gregor, so try to understand him. Put yourself in his place." Michiko pouted but nodded.

"Not bad, Blondie!" Gregor said with a smirk. "Maybe she'll—"

"As for you," Beth said, "my name is Beth, not 'Blondie'."

"But—"

Beth pointed at the guinea pig. "I'm only going to say this once, so listen. If you ever, and I mean ever, pull that kind of crap on me or Michiko again, I will dangle you by a bungee cord over a pit full of hungry cats. Get it?"

Gregor swallowed hard. "Got it."

"Good." Beth lowered her arm and restrained a sigh of relief. "Michiko, let's fill Gregor in. We need to get to work."

Ten minutes later, Michiko and Beth set off with Gregor for the alley near Leiber Lane. Michiko had her seeming on, and Beth was carrying the guinea pig in a purse she had gotten in a white elephant Christmas exchange and never used, in part because she hated purses but mostly because it was gaudy and shiny enough to blind the unwary. It was almost as big as Beth's kitchen and made of gold lame fabric inside and out, with golden sequins sewed all over in patterns that reminded people of eldritch Rorschach blots. Beth wished that she could have a seeming put on it, but she then realized it could probably repel them on its own.

When they reached the alley, Michiko checked to make sure they were alone, then snapped her fingers. Beth opened the purse, and Gregor stuck his head out. "About time, girl," he said. "I felt like Paris Hilton's dog in there."

"But cuter than either of them," Michiko said with a grin. "Beth, is the barrier still there?" Beth glanced over and nodded.

Gregor stared at the entrance. "Whoever crafted this was good," he said after a minute. "It's anchored, and very well-constructed."

"Can you break it?"

"I don't know. Put me down and stand back."

Beth set the purse on the ground facing the barrier, and she and Michiko moved away. Gregor stared in the distance and mumbled under his breath; it sounded half-Latin and half-Cyrillic. His muscles tensed, his fur stood on end. Then, the air seemed to vibrate, and there was a sound like a rubber band snapping. "Ha!" Gregor said. "I've still got it!"

"It does look like the barrier's gone," Beth said.

Michiko took a penny from her pocket and tossed it towards the entrance. It flew through, hit the sidewalk, and rolled several feet before tumbling to a stop. "Nice job, Gregor!" she said, holding up the caution tape for Beth. "Let's see what's hiding here. Gregor, look for magical traps or residue. Beth, check for seemings."

"Or," Beth said, "we could just look for the obvious clue." She pointed to a corner in the back of the alley.

Michiko walked over and picked up the dagger lying there; it had been concealed from view from the sidewalk by an overturned shopping cart. "Look at the hilt," she said; it was black and thick. "It's a hobgoblin weapon."

"It's almost too obvious," Beth said.

"I know. If the hobgoblins did this, they're really sloppy. But I think it's time to go have a chat just the same."

Chapter Six

The three-story warehouse was old and decrepit. Windows were broken, walls were covered in graffiti and pasted-on posters, and trash and weeds were everywhere. "This is where the hobgoblins live?" Beth said.

"Appearances." Michiko snapped her fingers, dispelling her seeming. "They want it to look bad on the outside so they'll be left alone, but they've cleaned up and remodeled the inside."

"Emigre gentrification, huh?"

"That's one way to put it." Michiko walked up to the warehouse door, which had been boarded up and padlocked. "Try not to wreck their seemings if you can." She knocked on the door.

After a moment, a bolthole opened in the door. "What do you want?" a scratchy voice asked.

"We're investigating a kidnapping," Michiko said.

"And you are?"

"They call me the Monkey Queen."

The bolthole slammed shut. There was a brief but loud discussion inside. Then, the door creaked open, even though the seeming held, making it look like the boards were still in place. Michiko and Beth quickly stepped in.

They were in a waiting room; another door to the side led to the main warehouse. Two hobgoblin guards were there, pointing their pikes at the women as the front door closed. "What brings you here, humans?" one guard said.

"I got lost," Michiko said. "I thought this was Costco." The guard swore in the hobgoblin tongue, which made it sound even angrier.

"Guards! Stand down!"

Beth turned and saw a hobgoblin woman standing in the doorway to the warehouse. Her skin was a softer red, her hair was short and gray, and she wore a brown toga-like robe with a black sash and a red belt. "So you're the Monkey Queen," she said.

"I am," Michiko said. "And these are my companions, Beth McGill and Gregor." Beth nodded; Gregor stuck his head out of the purse but kept quiet.

"I am called Amitya," the hobgoblin said. "I am the Speaker for the hobgoblin Emigres. I understand that you have urgent business to discuss."

"We do," Michiko said. "Is there an office?"

"This way." Amitya led them out of the waiting room.

They stepped into a large room with high ceilings, lit by a handful of windows and a few spotlights. A dozen hobgoblins were gathered there, sitting at tables or crossing the stone floor. Off to one side, a makeshift skylight let the sun in on a small stretch of grass and bushes. A handful of children were playing there, running madly about as an elderly hobgoblin matron tried to calm them down. On the far side of the room was a maze of crude plywood partitions, with many hallways and doors; Amitya led the humans to a door and waved them in.

The office was simply furnished, with a small desk and several rickety chairs. There was another hobgoblin sitting there; he was wearing a black tunic and trousers with a red belt and trim. "This must be the famous Monkey Queen," he said as he got to his feet.

"It is!" Michiko said. "Did you want my autograph?"

"Not particularly." He still extended a hand. "I am Vrech. I'm on the Hoblands Council."

Michiko's eyes widened. "Puck speaks highly of you," she said as they shook hands. "Maybe I should be asking for your autograph."

"Hardly." Vrech smiled slightly.

"So what brings you here?"

45

"I came to discuss the Emigre situation with Amitya. Who's your friend?"

"Beth McGill," she said. "I'm helping with this case." They shook hands.

"The Monkey Queen mentioned a kidnapping," Amitya said as they sat down.

Michiko nodded. "Puck's been abducted. All the evidence we have so far points to a hobgoblin gang as the culprits."

Amitya gasped. Vrech's expression darkened. "Tell me what you know, Monkey Queen," he said.

Michiko related her two earlier encounters with hobgoblins, Tierra's account of what happened, and their findings in the alley. She finished by pulling the hobgoblin dagger from her pocket and laying it on the desk.

Vrech stared at the dagger. "Monkey Queen...I know what the evidence shows. But I'm ready to swear, here and now, that we are being set up."

He stood up and began to pace the small room. "I have worked for decades to bring my people out of the darkness. We took the Hoblands by force centuries ago, and we'd lived by the sword and by treachery, but many years ago, leaders with foresight and will took the first steps towards ending that by signing the Compact with the Courts. We're trying to overcome our bad reputation, to be an example for the Outlands and beyond. But now...this..." He sat down hard.

"Could there be some mistake?" Amitya asked.

"I disrupted their seemings," Beth said. "They were deliberately disguising themselves as humans."

"And that would mark them as Emigres," Michiko said.

Amitya shook her head. "I can't imagine who here would do that. We've had troublemakers here, but they've never bothered anyone outside."

"I hate to say this," Vrech said, "but are we sure it wasn't Krexx?"

"Who?" Michiko asked.

"He's our resident sorcerer," Amitya said. "He specializes in mechanically-based magic. His devices help keep us powered and protected."

"Unfortunately, his behavior lately has been eccentric at best and belligerent at worst." Vrech shook his head. "He's become more frustrated with our conditions, both here and in the Hoblands."

"Maybe we should talk to him?" Beth said.

"He's not fond of strangers or humans," Amitya said, "but if it will help clear our names, we'll take you to see him."

They walked deeper into the warehouse. The partitions there formed a long hallway, and Beth could see hobgoblins walking along or going into their little rooms. "How many hobgoblins live here?" she asked.

"More than a hundred," Amitya said. "We've had a few new arrivals and a few babies lately."

They reached a door at the far end of the hallway. Amitya knocked on it. "Krexx?" she said. "We need to speak to you. It's official business."

There were footsteps, and then the door flew open. A hobgoblin in a long, stained and torn blue robe stood there, a triangular blue cap on his head, an odd-looking brass contraption in his hand. "Speaker Amitya! Councilor Vrech!" he said. "What brings—"

His gaze landed on Michiko, who grinned, and Beth, who smiled and raised a hand in greeting. "Humans!" he shouted, and he ducked back inside and slammed the door.

"That could have gone better," Beth said, lowering her hand.

"Of all the nerve!" Amitya threw the door open and stormed in, the others following.

The room was dimly lit, with tables and workbenches everywhere, all piled with spare parts, half-finished devices, and the occasional smoking or bubbling flask. Krexx was in a corner, one arm raised to shield his face. "Why are the humans here?" he shrieked. "Are they here to evict us? Or destroy us?"

"They're here to talk to you," Vrech said. "There was a kidnapping last night."

"Who?"

"Puck, the faerie Emigre."

Krexx lowered his arm. "Why should I care if a faerie was kidnapped?"

"Because it was apparently done by hobgoblins using seemings," Amitya said.

"Oh." Krexx calmed down. "Wasn't me. I don't do seemings. And I've been here for at least 24 hours. Gears don't reset on their own, you know."

"Are you sure?" Michiko asked. "They say you're good at whipping up devices that mimic spells." She pointed to a belt with a glowing brass buckle on a workbench. "Like that belt. What does it do?"

"Typical human," Krexx said with a sneer. "Always quick to assign blame."

"I just wanted to know—"

"Could have been new arrivals," Krexx said. "Could have been agents paid by Faerie. Could have been shapeshifters. But you're blaming me, after all I've done here!"

"She wasn't blaming you," Beth said, raising her hands as she took a step towards the sorcerer. "We just want to find our friend, that's all."

"That belt helps me levitate to the rafters to fix lights!" Krexx shouted, anger in his eyes. He pulled a brass rod, adorned with wires and crystals, from his robe and pointed it at Beth. "Why don't we see what this does?" he screamed. Beth stepped back and raised her arms to shield her face.

Michiko sprung across the room and knocked the rod from Krexx's hand. She grabbed him by his collar and glared at him. "You may have heard of me," she said. "I'm the Monkey Queen. And if you ever threaten Beth again, I will make you regret it."

"Monkey Queen." Amitya laid a hand on her shoulder. "I'll talk to him. I'm sorry about this."

Michiko nodded and released Krexx; he fell to the floor and covered his head. "We should probably go," she said.

"Shapeshifters?" Beth asked Michiko and Vrech as they walked back down the hall. "Would that mean werewolves or something?"

"Not this time," Michiko said. "Shapeshifters tend not to get along with each other. I can't imagine three of them working together."

"And why would they go through the training and the trouble to just take a hobgoblin form?" Vrech said. "I don't think they'd be willing to take on a weakness just for that."

"A weakness?" Beth asked.

"Yep!" Michiko said. "A shapeshifter has to take a weakness before they can learn how to take a new shape. It's a required part of the ritual. If that shape is a specific sentient being, they have to take a weakness related to that person's tastes."

"That still doesn't rule out some of the other possibilities Krexx mentioned," Beth said. "Like a band of rogues from the Hoblands."

"I know," Vrech said as they reached the door to the guard room. "I will make some inquires. But I hope both of you will keep an open mind on this, and not blame us unless there's solid proof that hobgoblins were behind the abduction."

"We will," Michiko said as the door opened. "We'll be in touch."

They walked away from the hobgoblin shelter in silence as the daylight faded. Michiko pouted as she stared at the ground. "So how many ways did I blow that one?" she said.

"Huh?" Beth said.

"Krexx wasn't a threat," Michiko said. "That rod wasn't charged. He just wanted us to go away."

"You didn't know that."

"She should have," Gregor said, sticking his head out of the gaudy purse. "Anyone with any sense could have seen that it was a bluff."

"Gregor!" Beth said.

"Beth, he's right." Michiko shook her head. "I should have known. What if I've pushed Krexx over the brink? The hobgoblins need him."

"Michiko…" Beth stopped and looked at her partner. "What's done is done. We can go back later and apologize if we need to. But you did what you thought you had to do to protect me, and I'm glad you did. Thanks." She smiled.

Michiko tried to return her smile. "You're welcome. I just wish—"

"Monkey Queen!"

She and Beth turned and saw a group of faeries, their seemings already removed, heading their way. One faerie walked ahead of the others. He was older and taller, and carried himself with a noble, arrogant air. His robe was red and gold, like the others, but shone as if real gold had been woven into the fabric. His ornate jewelry matched, right down to the diamond and ruby studded diadem he wore.

"Well, if isn't Duke Wrexham!" Michiko said. "What brings you to our sleepy little town? Slumming?"

"How droll," Wrexham said. "No, I came on a Court-related matter. But I bring good tidings!"

"You're leaving already?" Michiko said.

"Ah, another example of what humans mistakenly call 'humor'. No, I have come to tell you that your search is over."

"Thanks, but I'm not looking for a date tonight."

"Enough of your jokes!" the Duke shouted. "Behold! I have accomplished what the Monkey Queen could not!" He stepped aside and gestured. His men parted—

And Puck stepped out of the crowd, appearing to be none the worse for wear.

"Professor!" Beth ran past Michiko and Wrexham, but before she could reach Puck, two faerie soldiers cut her off. "Hey!" she said as they pushed her back.

"You'll have to forgive my men," the Duke said. "Puck has been through quite an ordeal."

"Aye," Puck said. "I am thankful that the Duke's men rescued me when they did."

"The kidnappers escaped," Wrexham said, "but we will track them down."

"And we won't need the help of an overrated, egotistical, self-proclaimed hero—"

"Huh?" Michiko said, blinking in surprise.

"—or a confused girl in way over her head—"

"What?" Beth said in a small, stunned voice.

"—to have our vengeance," Puck said.

Wrexham nodded. "We'll discuss this more tomorrow," he said to Puck. "Tonight, we feast to celebrate your freedom!"

The faeries turned to go. Wrexham looked back at Michiko and smiled cruelly. "Goodnight, Monkey Queen," he said. Puck also looked back; he said nothing, but his smile matched the Duke's.

Beth stared at him as they left. "Professor?" she said. "What happened to you? What happened?"

Michiko scowled. "I don't know, but I don't like it."

"Funny how that all worked out," Gregor said with a shrug. "Ah, well. You'll be taking me back to the pet store now, right?"

Beth and Michiko glared at him. "No," they said at the same time.

Chapter Seven

It was after dark by the time they returned to Beth's apartment. By then, Michiko had asked about staying there overnight again, and Beth had quickly agreed, still quietly worried about the ogre and the shadow bird from the night before. They had an extra-large Hawaiian pizza delivered, and Beth broke out and shared another dark chocolate bar from her stash. They talked all the while about Puck, but got no closer to understanding the change in his behavior.

Beth decided to lighten the mood, and pulled some of her *Doctor Who* DVDs off the shelf. She gleefully talked about the show to Michiko, who seemed interested, and Gregor, who buried himself in his bedding. They were halfway through "The Next Doctor" when there was a burst of music. "Is that your phone?" Beth asked Michiko.

"Yep," Michiko said as she pulled it from her pocket.

"What's the ringtone? It sounds familiar."

"'Last Train to Clarksville'. Could you pause the DVD? Thanks." As Beth thumbed the remote, Michiko answered her phone with "Hello?"

She listened for a minute, then sprung from the couch. "Where?" she said. "How long ago?...Got it. We're on our way."

Michiko ended the call and looked over at Beth. "What happened?" Beth asked.

"There's someone missing at the faerie settlement."

"Not Puck again?"

Michiko shook her head, a grim look in her eyes. "It's a baby," she said. "A faerie girl, four months old."

"Oh my God." Beth jumped up from the couch.

"They're desperate to find her. Gregor?"

The guinea pig popped out of his bedding. "We're going out this late?" he said.

"Sorry, but this job isn't regular business hours." Michiko glanced around the living room. "Beth?" she asked.

Beth came out of her bedroom, carrying Gregor's purse. "Had to get my jacket," she said. "It's going to be cold tonight." She glanced over at Michiko. "Ummm…you did want me to come, right?"

Michiko smiled. "Yeah, but I'm glad you volunteered. Bring a flashlight."

Michiko led Beth along the dirt trail they had taken that morning to get to Tierra's cottage. They continued past it, further up the trail, their way lit by moonlight poking through the trees. It was a chilly night, as Beth had expected, and she hoped that the fog would stay away a bit longer.

After a minute, Michiko veered left, into a thick copse of coast redwoods. She pushed her way through a clump of underbrush. As Beth followed, she could sense seemings around them, and she did her best to ignore them and leave them intact.

They stepped out of the underbrush. Beth's eyes widened.

They were in the outskirts of a small tent village. The tents were crafted from canvas, and while some were in bland colors, others were gaily painted or decorated with beads and silken trim. They had doors, and flaps that could open up for windows; some had wood frames, and a few flew banners that Beth guessed were from the residents' home Courts back on Faerie.

None of the residents were in sight, but in the light of the lanterns that lined the paths between the tents, Beth saw a clearing. Michiko led her there; as they went, they could hear a commotion.

The clearing served as a town square, and it was packed with faeries, some in their traditional clothing, some in outfits from second-hand stores.

They were gathered near a gnarled tree stump where a young faerie woman sat, her hands covering her face. Several other faeries were trying to comfort her, including a tall young man with haunted eyes who stood behind her, his hands resting on her shoulders.

One faerie broke away from the group and walked up to Michiko and Beth. He was bearded and heavy-set, wearing a plain green robe and, incongruously, a white wool hat. "Monkey Queen," he said. "I'm glad you could come so quickly. Who's your friend?"

"She's Beth McGill. Beth, this is Linden. He's the Mayor here."

"I had heard that you might have picked up a partner," Linden said as he shook Beth's hand. She bit off the impulse to say that it was still temporary; she knew there were bigger things to worry about.

Michiko nodded. "What info do you have?"

"Very little. The parents there, Larkin and Florence, took their eyes off the girl for a moment while she was playing outside. When they looked back, she was gone."

"Any witnesses? Any clues?"

"I'll tell you what I saw!" A tall, young faerie male in a red flannel shirt that matched his hair walked up to Michiko and Linden. "There were big footprints, left by someone wearing boots, leading into the woods!"

"Jasper—" Linden started to say.

"Yeah, big ones. Like the ones your friends made, Monkey Queen," Jasper said, face reddening with anger.

"That was a misunderstanding," Michiko said.

"Oh? How do we know that they're not at it again?"

"Stand down," Linden said to Jasper.

"Stand down?" Jasper clenched a fist. "One of our own is missing, and the best you can do is run to the humans to get help? Cry to them while the nien—"

"That's enough!" Linden locked eyes with Jasper.

"Fine." Jasper turned and stormed off, shouting, "So we'll let this Monkey Queen help? Like she did with finding Puck? We should have asked Duke Wrexham for help instead!"

"Why you—" Beth started to say. Michiko quietly shushed her.

Linden grimaced. "I apologize, Monkey Queen," he said. "He was out of line."

"Don't worry about it," Michiko said. "He's just blowing off steam. Did you follow up on the footprints?"

"We tried. The trail went cold after a few hundred yards. I've got twenty people searching the woods for her now."

Michiko nodded. "Jasper may have a point."

"About the nien?"

"It's as good a place to start as any. Let's go, Beth." Michiko turned and started towards the woods.

"Monkey Queen?"

She stopped and looked over to where Larkin and Florence were sitting. "We just looked away for a few seconds," Florence said in a trembling voice, "and she was gone. Please help us. Please find our baby." She lowered her head. Larkin, standing behind her, squeezed her shoulders gently.

"What's her name?" Michiko asked.

"Brooke," Larkin said.

Michiko nodded. "We'll find her. I promise."

As they headed deeper into the woods, Beth realized that Michiko had been quiet for several minutes. "You okay?" she asked.

"Yeah. Just thinking."

"About that jerk Jasper?" Beth felt her face redden with anger.

Michiko sighed. "I can't blame him for feeling the way he does. But I'm more concerned about the nien."

"Who?"

"The nien are an old, long-lived race. There's only a handful of them left, and a married couple live just a short walk from here. They're good people, but they can be shy around Emigres, and they get lonely. That led to them doing something…awkward a while back. They found a faerie toddler who had wandered off into the woods. They thought the kid had been abandoned, and brought her home to raise her."

"How did that get straightened out?" Beth asked.

"Um…" Michiko blushed. "I helped, actually. It was a mess, but I finally persuaded the nien to give the baby back to her parents. And calmed down the lynch mob."

"Lynch mob?"

"The nien had a bad reputation in the past. Many of them fought against the Monkey King during the last True Millennium. The faeries were ready to string them up first and ask questions later, and I'm worried they may react that way again. Anyway, we're here."

They had reached a good-sized cabin just off the trail. "Beth, try not to be too spooked by how they look," Michiko said. "They may seem frightening, but they're actually quite nice."

"Got it. Anything else?"

Michiko whistled, and her street clothes seeming appeared. "Red clothing scares them quite a bit," she told Beth. "You're not wearing anything red, are you?"

Beth double-checked her t-shirt; it was the same white print on black Pirate Festival shirt as it had been that morning. "Nope," she said.

"Not even…under there?" Michiko grinned.

"Pervert," Beth said, trying not to giggle as Michiko knocked on the door with her staff. There were muffled voices from inside, then heavy footsteps.

The door opened. Beth tried not to scream.

The nien was about seven feet tall and three feet wide. He had yellow hair and gray skin, and his face looked like a children's book illustration of a Chinese monster, all big ears and eyes and nose and lips. His fur-tipped tail poked out of his blue robe, swishing nervously. "Monkey Queen?" he asked in a voice that sounded like water rushing over gravel.

"Good evening, Terrible Tang," Michiko said with a courteous bow. "It's a pleasure to see you."

"The pleasure is mine." Tang returned the bow. "Who are your companions?"

"The furry one is Gregor, and the human is Beth McGill." The guinea pig grunted. Beth nodded and smiled, covering up that she was about to faint.

Terrible Tang nodded back at Beth. "Is this for business or pleasure?" he asked Michiko.

"Business, I'm afraid. May we come in?"

The nien nodded again and led the visitors in. The cabin was large, and all the furniture was oversized to fit the nien's proportions. There was another nien on the couch; Beth assumed it was female from the makeup and hairbows she wore. "Good evening, Monkey Queen," she said.

"Good evening, Frightful Fu. I apologize for intruding, but I need to discuss something with both of you."

"Go ahead," Tang said.

"Thank you." Michiko paused. "There's been a missing person report at the faerie encampment tonight."

"Puck?"

"This is different. It's a four month old faerie, a girl."

Tang's eyebrows jumped. He glanced over at Fu, who seemed shocked. "They think we did it, don't they?" he said.

"Some of them do," Michiko said.

"We didn't!" Tang shouted. "I swear we didn't! We've been here all night!"

"We made a big mistake once," Fu said, "but we know it was wrong."

"Okay. So…" Michiko pointed around the room. "Why is there a stuffed rabbit toy there? And a small blanket?"

The nien looked guiltily at each other. Then, Tang whistled.

A small white poodle trotted into the living room. He spotted Gregor and barked playfully. "Close the purse!" the guinea pig stage-whispered to Beth as he ducked back inside.

"Aw, what a cutie!" Beth said as the dog walked up to her. "What's his name?"

"Doggie," Fu said, smiling proudly.

"It's very…descriptive." Beth patted the dog as he sniffed the purse.

Michiko gave Tang a quizzical look. "He was abandoned in the woods," the nien said. "A human tied his leash to a tree and drove off. We couldn't just leave him there."

"Don't take him from us, Monkey Queen," Fu pleaded. "Please."

"I won't," Michiko said as Doggie sniffed her leg curiously. "Just take good care of him. Make sure he gets his checkups."

"We will," Tang said. He and Fu smiled with relief.

"Where did you find Doggie anyway?" Michiko bent down to pet the poodle.

"Right by the bridge," Tang said.

"Bridge?" Michiko snapped up straight.

"Yes, the footbridge over the creek. It's just up the trail."

Michiko nodded. "Beth? Gregor? Time to go."

"About time," Gregor muttered as Doggie barked again at his purse.

As soon as they had left the cabin, Michiko had snapped her fingers to remove her seeming, taken out her smartphone and made a call. "Linden?" she said. "I've got a lead. It's a hunch, but I think it's solid. Keep your people away from the nien, but if you don't hear from me in 15 minutes, start searching by the footbridge over the creek."

She hung up and picked up her pace. "What's so important about a footbridge?" Beth asked as she tried to keep up.

"Where there's a bridge," Michiko said, "there might be a troll."

"Troll?" Beth glanced nervously around the dark woods.

"They don't call themselves cannibals," Michiko said, "but that's because they don't eat each other. Anything else is fair game for them."

"Even faeries?"

"Unfortunately. And babies are like candy for them."

Beth swallowed. "Where would a troll have come from?"

"Faerie, through the auldgate. Trolls there are trying to clean up their image, like hobgoblins, but some have backslid. But we're here." Michiko pointed with her staff at a small bridge over a creek. "I'll search in the woods. Take Gregor and look around by the bridge. And if you see a troll, don't be a hero. Scream to get my attention and run away."

"Like you need to tell me to do that," Beth said. She took out her flashlight and started away from the trail, down the hill towards the creek.

After a few minutes and lots of careful steps, Beth reached the creek bank, a short distance from the bridge. "Gregor?" she said, opening the purse.

Gregor stuck his head out. "You're not going to put the baby in this ugly thing if you find her, are you?" he grumbled.

"That would be child abuse," Beth said as she switched her flashlight on. "Do you have any troll detection spells?"

"I prefer 'keep the troll from eating me' spells."

"That actually makes sense...wait." Beth squinted. "Do you see something over there?"

"I do. It may be a fire."

Beth nodded and moved as quickly and quietly as she could. In a minute, she and Gregor reached what appeared to be a crude campsite. There was a small fire that had almost burnt itself out, a primitive tent, and a pile of trash that Beth tried not to look at. "He must have gone to get more wood," Beth said.

"Or a main course," Gregor said.

"That's a scary thought—hang on." Beth headed for the tent.

"Are you mad, girl?"

"I thought I heard something in here." Beth pulled the flap aside and shone her flashlight into the tent.

There was a dirty, disgusting blanket on top of a stained mattress. Lying on the blanket was a baby, obviously faerie from the ears. Her crying was muffled by the cloth tied around her mouth. "What kind of loser puts a gag on a baby?" Beth said as she picked up the little girl.

"The kind who doesn't want it to be heard," Gregor said.

"Well, not tonight," Beth said as she carried the baby from the tent. "You must be Brooke," she said as she slipped the gag off. "It's okay now, sweetie. We've got you."

Brooke kept crying. "Check the diaper," Gregor said.

"I don't think that's it," Beth said as she gently rocked the baby. "She's probably hungry, poor thing."

"Or she just saw something that frightened her," Gregor said, suddenly trembling.

Beth turned pale. "Please tell me that was meant as a joke."

An angry bellow drowned out Gregor's reply. Beth spun around and gasped.

The troll was eight feet of muscle and blood-red hair, with a big bulbous nose and ears and a mouthful of sharp teeth, wearing only a crude loincloth and boots. He lifted a club and, with an angry roar, charged at Beth and the baby. Beth had her back to the tent and was boxed in; she took a deep breath and screamed, "Michiko! Help!"

The troll swung his club, but it stopped and bounced back. "Barrier spell," Gregor shouted; with her second sight, Beth could see the faint outline in front of them. "I'll try to hold it, but—" The troll swung again, with the same result. "—he's strong. Keep screaming!"

"Help!" Beth yelled as the troll kept hammering at the barrier. "Michiko! Troll! Michiko, help!" Brooke cried and wriggled in her arms.

"Try to move sideways," Gregor said as he panted. "Maybe we can run away if we can get past the tent." Beth nodded and edged along the tent, the barrier spell following her. She kept shouting, but she could feel her voice going.

The troll snarled, raised his club and swung with all his might. It hit the barrier, and there was a flash of white light. "Gregor!" Beth said.

"I couldn't hold him," he said. "Too strong. Out of practice." He shook his head. "I'm sorry, girl."

"Run!" Beth tossed Gregor's purse aside to give him a chance to escape and crouched down, shielding Brooke as best as she could. She looked up and screamed as the troll smiled cruelly and raised his club.

Then, he stopped and roared in pain as a staff hit him on the side of the head. He turned.

"Now that I have your attention…" The Monkey Queen spun her staff around. "I'll give you one chance." She pointed her staff at the troll. "Back away from these people, swear off eating intelligent beings, and return to Faerie. If you do that, I'll let you leave with all your teeth. Deal?"

The troll smiled and started to drool. "Tasty human girl!" he said. "Eat you first! Save baby for dessert!"

Michiko made a face. "Oh, I am so not buying your diet book," she said as the troll charged. He swung his club at her; she leaped high in the air to avoid the blow. As she came down, she hit the troll again on the side of the head with her staff.

He growled and swung again. Michiko blocked the club with her staff, but the troll pushed harder, and his pressure bent her down. She glanced back at Beth and jerked her head to the side. "Get Brooke out of here," she mouthed. Beth nodded and stood up, carefully holding Brooke. She then grabbed Gregor's purse and started to back away, towards the hillside.

The troll saw her moving away and stood up straight, pulling his club back. With his pressure gone, Michiko stumbled to her knees. The troll then threw his club at Beth.

Michiko quickly spun her staff in her hand over her head, then flung it at the club. The spinning staff caught the club just before it reached Beth and knocked it aside, both weapons skidding to a stop near Beth's feet.

Michiko tried to stand, but the troll grabbed her and lifted her off the ground, high enough so that they were face-to-face. He then wrapped his arms around her and tightened them, crushing her against his chest. "Smush you!" he said as she tried to break free. "Eat you! Eat baby!" He laughed cruelly.

Anger flared in Michiko's eyes. She pushed her head forward and up and bit down hard on the troll's bulbous nose.

He shouted in pain and dropped Michiko, grabbing at his nose. She landed on her feet and punched the troll in the stomach. As he doubled over, gasping for breath, she stuck her right hand out to one side. Her staff rose into the air and flew into her hand like a pin jumping onto a magnet.

Michiko then hit the troll in one knee with her staff, then the other. As the troll reeled, she jumped high in the air. She swung her staff over her head and down as she descended, hitting the troll hard over the top of his head. He collapsed, out cold.

Michiko landed on her knees, coughing and spitting. She pulled a bottle of water from her pocket and rinsed out her mouth. "Are you okay?" Beth said hoarsely as she ran over with Brooke.

"I bit his nose!" Michiko shouted. "It was the most disgusting thing I have ever had to do in my life!"

"Really?"

"Two words: troll boogers."

"Oh, ick." Beth tried not to gag.

"Here." Michiko stood up and handed Beth the water. "Sounds like you could use this."

Beth somehow managed to hold Brooke in one hand and the water in the other, and finished the bottle. "Thanks," she said. "And Michiko?"

"Yeah?"

"Thanks for saving my butt again." Beth smiled.

"You're welcome," Michiko said, blushing faintly as she smiled back. "How's the baby?"

"Nodding off. She's all cried out, the poor thing. Did you want to hold her? My arms are getting tired."

"Sure!" Michiko carefully took the baby from Beth. "Hi, Brooke!" she said as she gently swayed back and forth. "Such a little sweetie!"

"Awww," Beth said to herself as she watched.

"Gregor?" Michiko said as she walked with the baby.

The guinea pig, eyes half-closed and whiskers drooping, stuck his head out of the purse. "Yes?" he said.

"Good work."

"What good work? I couldn't stop the troll!" Gregor said.

"But you did hold him off until I got here. Thanks for that." Michiko smiled.

"Yeah," Beth said with a grin. "You did great, Gregor."

"So did you, Beth."

"Huh?" Beth said, her eyes widening with surprise. "All I did was scream!"

"And find this camp," Michiko said. "And Brooke."

"Oh. Right."

"And the screaming was excellent! Great volume, and just the right amount of panic."

"Gee, thanks," Beth said sarcastically. "I'll remember that for next time." She glanced up the hill towards the trail. "Someone's coming."

Linden was hurrying down the hill, followed by half a dozen armed faeries. They stopped and gaped in surprise. "We had a troll here?" the mayor asked.

Michiko nodded. "Beth found Brooke in that tent. I got here in time to stop the troll."

"Is it…?"

"Still alive. I'd recommend chaining him up and sending him back to Faerie, with a note that says 'baby eater'. Let them deal with him."

Linden nodded and turned back to the others, who surrounded the still-unconscious troll. As they did, two more faeries ran down the hill. "Monkey Queen!" Larkin shouted as he and Florence stopped short of the troll. "Is—is she—"

Michiko smiled and walked up to them. "She's just fine." She gave Brooke to Florence, who burst into tears as she held the sleeping baby close to her. Larkin stood behind them, one arm around his wife's waist, the other stroking the baby's head gently, tears on his cheeks.

"Awww," Beth said again with a wide smile. Gregor stuck his head out of her purse and snorted. "Oh, come on!" Beth said to him. "Doesn't this make you feel warm and fuzzy inside?"

"I'm a guinea pig," he grumbled. "I'm too warm and fuzzy as it is."

Larkin and Florence looked up. "Monkey Queen…thank you," Larkin said.

"Yes, thank you," Florence said. "How can we ever repay you?"

"She's a little sweetie," Michiko said. "Love her with all your heart. That's all."

Larkin nodded. "We will." He and Florence turned their attention back to their baby.

Michiko walked back to Beth and Gregor. "Time to go," she said to them. "Beth, listen. Do you have…"

"Mouthwash?" she said. "Sure. Use as much as you want."

"Thanks!"

They walked back up the hill to the trail. When they reached it, Michiko stopped. "Beth?" she asked. "One more thing."

"Yeah?"

"If you ever wonder why I do what I do…" Michiko pointed down at Brooke and her parents. "That's why." She smiled warmly.

Chapter Eight

Michiko was nodding off by the time they returned to Beth's apartment. She used half a bottle of Beth's mouthwash, then curled up on the couch and quickly fell asleep. By then, Gregor was already snoring in his cage.

Beth went to bed, but for the second night in a row, she lay awake, staring at the ceiling. Her thoughts raced, replaying everything that had happened; it had been quite a Saturday. She kept coming back to Puck's behavior after he had been rescued; she was still confused by it, and she felt hurt and rejected as well.

Beth knew she still hadn't made a decision, committed either way on whether she would stick it out with the Monkey Queen. She was glad that Michiko hadn't pressured her. But deep down inside, Beth was scared out of her mind. And having the time of her life in spite of it.

Sunday morning finally came, and Beth staggered out of her bedroom to see Michiko was already awake and holding a coffee cup. "Good morning!" Michiko said, smiling cheerfully.

"Mrph," Beth said as she headed into the kitchen. "Thanks for making the coffee again. How's Gregor?"

"Eating breakfast," Michiko said. Beth glanced over as she fixed her coffee. The guinea pig was ignoring them as he munched on a stack of alfalfa.

Beth sipped her coffee. "So…cold pizza for us?"

"Save it for lunch. I've got a place we can go."

"Food decent?"

"Better than that. And we might see Puck there." Michiko grinned and finished her coffee.

Beth's heart jumped. "He likes early breakfasts," she said. "I'd better shower so we can get going." She took one last gulp of coffee and headed for her bedroom.

"They'll let you wear your bunny slippers there!" Michiko said.

"You wish!" Beth said as she closed the bedroom door.

Gregor shook his head. "They're both mad," he muttered through a mouthful of alfalfa.

Michiko led Beth, who was carrying Gregor in the gaudy purse, on a walk that took them to the outskirts of town. They eventually came to a dirt road that dead-ended in front of an old, abandoned and somewhat worn-down barn that sat atop a small hill. "This is it?" Beth asked. "We have to gather our own eggs for breakfast?"

"Have you forgotten about the hobgoblin shelter and Grandmother Fox's garden?" Michiko said with a grin as she snapped her fingers.

"Oh. Oh!"

"Well put."

Then, they saw a middle-aged man wearing business casual coming up the road. "Monkey Queen?" he asked.

Michiko folded her arms. "I like to see who I'm really dealing with," she said.

"Of course." He gestured before Beth could blink, and his seeming vanished. "Good morning to both of you," Vrech said.

"Good morning." Michiko relaxed. "What brings you here?"

"Apparently, Puck has been found."

"He has. We ran into him last night."

"He was with Duke Wrexham," Beth said.

"Did Wrexham give any indication of how or where Puck was found?" the hobgoblin asked.

"He was too busy boasting."

"Yes, that sounds like the Duke." Vrech paused. "I'm worried that they'll find a way to pin the blame on us. I'm still convinced that no hobgoblins were involved."

"So who would have done it?" Michiko asked. "And why?"

"I can't answer that. But I do know that Wrexham is out to take advantage of this situation. He has always coveted the Hoblands for his own. This could be his first step to fulfilling his ambition. Besides, ask yourselves this: What would our motive have been?"

"Revenge?" Michiko said.

"Ransom?" Beth said.

"Bargaining chip?" Gregor said.

"All valid points," Vrech said. "That's why I'm asking for your help."

"To find out who was behind this?" Michiko said.

"Yes. If we get pinned with the blame, everything we've worked for will be ruined, and so could the Hoblands." Vrech looked away. "I'm not too proud to ask for help for my people. Please, Monkey Queen. Please help us."

After a long moment, Michiko nodded. "I'll do what I can. I can't promise anything, but I'll try."

Vrech extended a hand. "That's all I could ask for," he said. "Thank you."

"I'll be in touch." Michiko shook his hand. The hobgoblin turned and headed away from the barn, gesturing as he did, his seeming coming back on.

"Do you think that any hobgoblins were behind this?" Beth asked.

Michiko shook her head. "The more I think about it, the more I'm convinced that they're not."

"Yeah, there's one thing that's been bothering me."

"What's that?"

"You know the barrier spell across the alley? The one that Gregor dispelled?"

"I know what you're getting at, girl," the guinea pig said. "I'm not familiar with whatever spell that was, or with hobgoblin magic, but I didn't see any device there that could have generated that barrier."

"So that rules Krexx out," Michiko said. "I wonder…"

Before she could continue, the barn door opened. "Professor!" Beth shouted. She handed Gregor and purse to Michiko and ran up the road towards Puck as he stepped outside.

Puck raised an eyebrow as Beth approached him. "Yes?" he said.

"Well…" Beth quickly gathered her thoughts. "I wanted to say that it's good to see you. And that I'm glad you're okay."

He nodded. "And I have something to say to you, girl." *Girl and not lass?* Beth thought as Puck said, "Get away from the Monkey Queen now, while you can. Before it's too late."

"What?" Beth turned pale.

"What did I just tell you, girl?" Puck said.

"But you said the other night—"

"Listen to what I'm telling you now! She is trouble! What has she done for you? Stop being a fool."

Beth shook her head. "Professor, she saved my life! She's—"

"She'll lead you to your doom, you idiot," Puck spat out. "You're not ready for this. Go back to your classes. Maybe you'll survive."

"But Professor—" Beth took a step towards Puck. He grabbed her arm and pushed her to one side. He walked away without another word, past Michiko and Gregor, down the dirt road and out of sight.

There was a weather-beaten wood bench by the side of the road. Beth sat down hard on it and stared at the ground, her eyes stinging. Michiko set Gregor's purse down and walked over to the bench. "Are you—" she started to say.

"Am I all right?" Beth said. "Do I look all right?"

"I…"

Beth looked up at Michiko, her face flushed with anger. "I'm not all right!" she shouted. "I just had a good friend—and he's only a friend, so shut up, Gregor—call me an idiot and a fool, and push me away! And he made it sound like it was my fault. Maybe," she said with bitterness, "this wouldn't have happened if I had never met you. Maybe he'd still be the same."

She stared at the ground again. Gregor ducked inside the purse. Michiko looked away sadly. "Do you really think that's true?" she asked. "Do you really believe that?"

"Only…" Beth swallowed. "Only the part of me that hurts like Hell."

Michiko looked back as Beth continued, "I don't have a lot of friends. I lost touch with the people I knew in high school when I came out here to college, I don't really know anyone here, every roommate I've ever had here bailed or flaked out, and my webfriends aren't there to give me their time and a pep talk when I do bad on a test or my day sucks." Her voice cracked. "Puck was the only one around who would. And now…" She took her glasses off and wiped her eyes.

Michiko took a package of tissues from her pocket and handed them to Beth. "Thanks," Beth said.

When Beth had composed herself, Michiko knelt in front of her. "Beth," she said, "I don't know what happened to Puck either. Maybe being kidnapped changed him, or maybe there's some other reason he's acting the way he is. But he's my friend too, and I want to find out what's going on. If you want to get out now, I understand, but I hope you'll stick it out."

Beth nodded. "Okay. I'm still in, then."

"Okay." Michiko stood and turned away.

"Michiko? Wait a minute." Beth stood up as Michiko looked back. "I'm sorry," she said, her face getting redder still. "I really am. I shouldn't have gone off on you like that. I know it's not your fault. You've done so much for me already, and you don't deserve to have me yelling at you. I'm sorry."

Michiko smiled. "Thanks, Beth. Come on, let's get breakfast." Beth nodded and managed a faint smile of her own as she picked up Gregor's purse.

Michiko had given her a hint, so Beth didn't expect to walk into the barn and see stables and bales of hay. Still, she was surprised by what she saw.

Inside the barn was a restaurant. There were sturdy wooden tables of various sizes and shapes, all surrounded by comfortable-looking chairs. There were booths along the walls, a large long couch against the far wall by a curtained doorway, and a coffee and pastry stand near the door; the fruit-filled danishes and heavily-iced cinnamon rolls made Beth's mouth water. Windows lined the walls, letting in the morning sun. The sights, sounds and smells of breakfast filled the air.

"Michiko," Beth asked, "there weren't this many windows outside, were there?"

"It's the seemings," Michiko said. "The ones here are so old and protected, even ten of you couldn't disrupt them."

"Okay. So what's the deal with this place?"

"It's—"

"Michiko!"

A short young woman with wild red hair, pointed ears and candycane-striped stockings dodged customers and tables and ran up to Michiko, giving her a hug. She wore purple eye shadow that matched her earrings and her dress, which she wore an apron over. It also matched the butterfly-like wings that poked through slits in the back of her dress. "Where have you been!" she said as she let Michiko go. "We've missed you!"

"Rogue wizards don't hunt themselves!" Michiko said.

"No kidding! Who's your friend?"

"Beth McGill. Beth, this is Mandy."

"You finally found a partner?" the waitress asked.

"I'm...auditioning, you could say," Beth said.

"I know all about that," Mandy said with a sigh. "Anyway, welcome to the Wonderland Diner and Tavern."

"Tavern?"

"It's in the back, and you will get carded," Mandy said. "Your favorite table's open, Michiko. Two?"

"And a child seat for the guinea pig," Michiko said.

"Guinea pig?" Mandy asked. "He's in that thing Beth's carrying?"

"It's a purse."

"Huh. I thought someone had skinned C-3PO. Come on."

Beth followed the pixie, but stopped when a faerie walked up to her and Michiko. It took Beth a moment to recognize Jasper, who had angrily confronted them the night before. "Monkey Queen?" he said.

"Yes?" Michiko said.

"I wanted to apologize for my behavior last night." Jasper lowered his head. "I was wrong."

Michiko nodded. "I understand," she said. "We were all under a lot of stress. How's Brooke?"

"She's doing fine." The faerie paused. "Florence is my sister, and Brooke is my niece. Thank you for saving her."

"You're welcome," Michiko said with a smile. "I'm glad I could help." She extended a hand, and Jasper shook it before turning and leaving. Michiko looked back at Beth; she smiled in turn as they headed for a table in the center of the restaurant.

As they sat down and settled in, Beth was able to get a good look at the other patrons. She and Michiko were the only humans there. Faeries were seated all over the restaurant, most wearing clothes that would only be considered casual by their standards; Beth recognized some from the settlement, and was surprised that a few of the others wore ornate Asian-style outfits. A dozen dwarves were eating heartily around a large round table, and three pixies sat nearby, wings fluttering as they shared scones and gossip. There was also a trio of what appeared to be short-haired werewolves snarling at each other over the last piece of bacon, two turquoise humanoids in black and white robes sipping orange juice and, in a corner, a giant reptilian…something reading the Sunday comics.

A short young male with skinny limbs and fingers, an oval-shaped face and large pointy ears walked up to the table. He had dark skin, bushy black hair, a grease-stained t-shirt and jeans, and a pair of goggles hanging around his neck. He grabbed a chair, swung it around, and sat down with his arms resting on the back. "Michiko," he said with a slight grin.

"Mec!" Michiko beamed.

"How does it go?"

"Saving the world, same as always. How about you?"

"Calibrating crystals, same as always. Who's your friend?"

"Beth McGill."

"New partner?" Mec asked as they shook hands.

"Auditioning," Beth said. "You're a mechanic?"

"Better than that. I'm a gremlin."

"Not like in those movies, I hope."

"Those movies—" Mec made a "tch" sound and waved his hand dismissively. "Michiko, you haven't told her a thing, have you?"

"I did!" Michiko said. "I wanted to tell her about you guys last night, but she made me watch some TV show named *Doctor What* instead."

"*Doctor Who*, you mean," Mec said, cutting off Beth's reply.

"Are you a fan?" Beth asked, her eyes lighting up.

"It's a good show, but I wish they'd bring back *Eureka*."

"How about *Chip and Dale's Rescue Rangers*?" Mandy asked as she returned to the table, carrying two menus and a high chair. She set the chair down and handed the menus to Michiko and Beth.

"How about you and *Winx Club*?" Mec said.

"Now, now," Mandy said as she bent down and gave Mec a peck on the cheek. "You know I'm a Tinker Bell girl." She hurried off.

Beth opened Gregor's purse and set the guinea pig in the high chair. "About time, girl," he grumbled. "I was starting to go blind in there."

"A talking guinea pig," Mec said.

"And a master of stating the obvious," Gregor said.

"Forgive me. I was hypnotized by your purse."

"Another indignity."

"So, Mec," Beth said, "what was Michiko supposed to be telling me?"

"About us. About this place." Mec gestured to take in the whole cafe. "Everyone here except for you three is an Emigre."

"From Faerie?"

"Mostly," Mec said, "except for Sam there in the corner and a handful of others. Most of us have to try to fit into human society at some point, so we put on our seemings and pretend. We all need a place to unwind and be ourselves, though, so we come here. It's a no-seeming zone, and a no-conflict zone, so we can relax and enjoy the company."

"And the free Wi-Fi!" Michiko said.

"And the cute waitresses!" Mec said as Mandy walked past. She rolled her eyes and tried not to smile.

"So you two..." Beth started to say.

"Are you familiar with the term 'sexual dimorphism'?"

"Isn't that illegal in some states?" Michiko said with a grin.

"Pixies and gremlins are the same species?" Beth said.

Mec nodded. "Pixies are always female, gremlins are always male. Pixies always have the wings, and usually have some creative talent."

"And gremlins get the mechanical ability?"

"And the good looks." Mec grinned.

"So how did you get left out?" Mandy said as she came back to the table, coffeepot and two mugs in hand. The gremlin stuck out his tongue at her as she set the mugs down. "Coffee okay for you?" she asked Beth.

"God, yes," Beth said, reaching for the cream and sugar.

"How about me?" Mec asked.

"You need to get going," Mandy said. "You're late."

"No, I'm not." The gremlin checked his watch. "Oh. Yes, I am."

"As usual."

"Hush." Mec stood up. "Michiko, good to have you back. Beth, nice to meet you. Gregor, get a better purse."

"Mec, get to work."

Mec kissed Mandy. "See you when you get off."

"Bye, sweetie."

"Bye, sugarplum." Mec left, passing a quartet of dwarves on his way out. Mandy grabbed menus and hurried over to them.

"So," Michiko asked Beth, "how's the coffee?"

Beth took a sip. Her eyes widened. "It's...it's good!"

"I know!"

"Restaurant coffee isn't supposed to be this good." Beth took another sip. As she did, she heard grumbling from a nearby table. She looked over and saw two men there, though she quickly realized that "men" was not quite accurate. One was easily seven feet tall, two feet taller than the other. They both had greasy black hair and big bulbous ears and noses, reminding Beth of the troll from the night before.

The shorter one looked up, saw Beth, and grimaced. "Dirty Earthling," he said, looking away. "They'll let anyone in here nowadays." The bigger one nodded.

Michiko muttered under her breath and started to stand, but Mandy was behind her, laying a hand on her shoulder. "I'm sorry," she said quietly to Beth. "I'll talk to them." Beth nodded as Michiko sat down, tight-lipped.

"Do you know those losers?" Beth asked Michiko.

"They're a couple of grifters," she said. "Their mother was a faerie, and their father was a troll. They're called Big Jake and Little Jake."

"What, did their mother run out of names?"

"They're twins."

Beth raised an eyebrow. "You have got to be—"

"MONKEY QUEEN!"

Beth froze in her chair and turned white. Gregor's fur stood on end.

A monster had burst out of the kitchen and was headed for their table. He was taller than Big Jake, purple with flaring red eyes and sharp fangs, fiery red hair, muscles everywhere, and huge bat-like wings. "Michiko!" he growled in the deepest voice Beth had ever heard.

Michiko stood up. "Yes?" she said with a grin.

"Where in the world have you been?" he asked. "We've missed you!" He gave Michiko a tremendous hug, which she eagerly returned. Beth and Gregor both sighed with relief.

"I've been busy! Bad guys don't hunt themselves!" Michiko pulled free and sat down.

"Who are these?"

"This is Beth McGill. Beth, this is Aloysius Alphonsus. He's the head chef here."

"Hello!" Aloysius said, smiling as he shook Beth's hand. She nodded, feeling too stupid to say anything; in her panic, she'd missed the chef's hat and apron he was wearing.

"And this is Gregor," Michiko said.

"Ooh! A guinea pig! He doesn't bite, does he?"

"I can talk, you know," Gregor snapped.

"That may be worse," Beth said.

"Beth," Aloysius asked. "What brings you here?"

"She's my new partner!" Michiko said with a grin.

"On this case, anyway," Beth said. "We'll see how it goes after that."

"What are you working on?" Aloysius said.

"We're trying to figure out what happened to Puck."

Aloysius's face fell. "I wish I knew," he said, shaking his head.

"You know him?"

"Almost everyone here knows Puck. Every Sunday, for years, he's come here for breakfast. He never sits by himself; he either brings company, or he sits with someone who's already here. And he always orders the same thing—the Flaming Pits of Hades omelet."

"That sounds like something he'd order," Beth said. "Just being near his food is almost too spicy for me to handle."

"I know! So today, he comes in by himself, asks for a menu, and sits by himself. He's quiet, and I couldn't blame him with all he's been through. So I thought I'd do him a favor, and I whip up his favorite, with extra jalapenos. And then he orders—"

"A Belgian waffle," Mandy said as she walked up to the table. "With whipped cream and blueberries."

"The omelet's still under the heat lamp," Aloysius said with a heavy sigh.

"Shouldn't you be in the kitchen?"

"But Clyde's back there—"

"It's Sunday!" Mandy said. "We're busy! And more dwarves just came in!"

"Have they ordered yet?" Aloysius asked.

"No."

"Has Michiko ordered yet?"

"No."

"Well, let's take care of that," Aloysius said. "What'll you have, Michiko?"

"Pancakes!" she said with a big smile.

"Big stack with fruit on the side?"

"Yep!"

"And you, Gregor?"

"I ate already," the guinea pig said.

"I'll fix you a little dessert, then. You'll like it. Beth?"

Beth turned red. "I've been so busy taking this in, I haven't even looked at the menu," she said. Michiko giggled.

"Try me," Aloysius said.

"Okay." Beth thought for a moment. "Ham and cheese omelet? Just a plain one, not like one of the Professor's?"

Aloysius nodded. "That comes with hot potato chunkies and your choice of toast."

"What do you recommend?"

"Well..." He bent down and whispered to Beth, "Just between you and me, we have a delicious sourdough English muffin."

"And blueberry jam?"

Aloysius straightened up. "Freshly made."

"Awesome!" Beth grinned. "Let's do this."

Aloysius beamed and collected the menus. Then, Mandy cleared her throat. Aloysius grinned sheepishly and handed her the menus. "Kitchen. Now," the waitress said.

"Alright, alright!" Aloysius moved quickly away from the table, wincing in pain as Mandy whacked him on the rump with the menus. "That hurts, you know," he said as the kitchen doors closed behind him.

Mandy hurried up to the front and put the menus away. As she did, a woman walked in and exchanged a few words with her. She had long gray curly hair and glasses with large round lenses and was wearing a purple sweater, red sweatpants, floppy hiking boots and hat, and a backpack and a shoulder bag. She was, to Beth's surprise, human.

She glanced quickly around the cafe and spotted Michiko. "Hello!" she shouted.

"Hiiii!" Michiko jumped out of her chair as the woman hurried over. They hugged.

"Where have you been?" the woman asked. "What have you been up to?"

"The usual," Michiko said, grinning. "Mary, this is Beth McGill. Beth, Mary Crimble."

Mary and Beth shook hands. "New partner?" Mary asked.

"We're working on Puck's case," Beth said.

"I thought they found him already."

"Long story."

"Join us!" Michiko said.

"Can't," Mary said. "I've got a walking tour in half an hour. I'm just getting pastries and coffee. Isn't the coffee here the best?"

"It is pretty good—"

"I'm leading a tour of the woods. It's the time of year for ghost stories, so I'll be telling a few along the trail. And did they catch the hobgoblins yet?"

"Not yet, but—"

"Wait. Funny story. Did you know there used to be another auldgate to Faerie here in town?"

"No!" Michiko said. "Do tell!"

"I will!" Mary said. "You know about the one in the woods, but the other one is right in the center of town. Right in the center of Paulsen Plaza, in fact."

"Where did it lead to?"

"From what I understand, it let out right by where the hobgoblins wound up settling. It was sealed during all that mess a long time ago, of course. Did you order the pancakes again?"

"Yep!"

"I knew it! You'll like the food here, Beth. Oh, here's mine! Thank you!" Mary said as Mandy handed her a paper bag and a large coffee. "Gotta run! Or eat and run! Or walk! Bye!"

"See you next week!" Michiko said with a smile. Beth nodded.

Mary waved as she headed for the door. "I hope they do something about the rodent problem here," she said out loud to herself.

"Michiko…?" Beth said.

"She's a friend of Puck's," Michiko said. "That's why."

"'Rodent problem'," Gregor muttered. "Bah!"

As Mary left, a faerie in red and gold hurried in. He went to Mandy and whispered to her; she rolled her eyes and pointed to the kitchen. He bowed and headed there, passing Michiko and Beth.

"One of Wrexham's men," Michiko said. "What's he up to now?"

"No good, I'll wager," said a faerie sitting by herself at a small table; several other diners murmured their agreement. She had wavy black hair and was dressed in a black turtleneck sweater and matching slacks. She had a cup of tea in front of her, and was reading a very old-looking book.

"Better him than some clueless Earthling!" Little Jake said with a sneer. Big Jake laughed.

The laughter stopped as Mandy charged towards them. "That's enough!" she said. "I already warned you once. Keep it up and you're out of here."

"We were just having fun, Mandy!" Little Jake said.

"Not here you don't," the pixie said, folding her arms.

"Yeah, whatever. Where's our breakfast?"

"You haven't paid for last Sunday's breakfast!"

"Next week, like I told you. Now," Little Jake said, "be a good little girl and get us—"

"Gentlemen." The Jakes looked over to where the faerie who had criticized Wrexham sat. "I am trying to read," she said. "Your blather is not helping. Be quiet, or else." Little Jake gulped and nodded, and took a sudden interest in the wood patterns in his table.

"Thanks, Scylla," Mandy said quietly. The faerie nodded and resumed her reading.

"Nice work there," said a faerie at a table near Scylla's. He had olive skin and curly brown hair, and was foppishly dressed, from his purple coat and frilled shirt to his buckled boots, which were resting on the table as he leaned back in his chair. *Give him the right hat*, Beth thought, *and he could pass for the Fifth Musketeer.*

"You shouldn't have your boots on the table, Windsor," Scylla said without looking up from her book.

"Ah, fair lass, I know where these boots should be."

"I suspect 'under Scylla's bed' is the answer."

"Smart and beautiful!" Windsor smiled and winked.

"Mandy?" Scylla said as the waitress walked by. "Could I get a glass of water?"

"Are you going to dump it on Windsor's head?" Mandy asked, eyebrow raised.

"If necessary, yes."

"Extra ice it is, then. And get your boots off the table, Windsor." He pouted but complied.

"Best show in town," Michiko said to Beth.

"Is that the same Windsor who—" Beth started to say.

"Yep. Hey, Windsor!"

He glanced at Michiko. "Yes?"

"You haven't told me how Tierra's doing."

"You haven't asked. I found a safe house for her. She's doing fine, but she's been asking after Puck."

"Could you keep her there?" Michiko asked. "For another day or so?"

Windsor raised an eyebrow. "Even though they've found Puck?"

"Let's not take any chances. Whoever did it is still out there."

Windsor sighed. "Fine. 24 hours more."

Michiko smiled. "Windsor! Is this 'safe house' your living room?"

He shrugged. "It was the best I could do on short notice. I was lucky to get away from her and get here today, and I still need to bring her back a veggie scramble."

"Thanks, Windsor! I owe you one."

He nodded as Wrexham's agent emerged from the kitchen and hurried out of the restaurant. "What would Wrexham want with a cook?" Beth asked.

"I bet it has something to do with Puck," Michiko said.

"Yeah. They were so buddy-buddy last night." Beth made a face.

"Scylla?" Michiko said.

The faerie looked up from her book. "Yes, Michiko?"

"Was Puck ever friendly with Wrexham?"

"Far from it."

"No surprise there," Beth said.

"Puck worked for Wrexham very briefly," Scylla said, "and it did not end well. If Puck ever had to choose between eating live scorpions or going back to work for Wrexham, I think he would have picked the scorpions."

"With hot sauce."

"Obviously."

"Thanks!" Michiko said.

Scylla nodded and returned to her reading as Mandy came by, carrying four plates, two big and two small. "Here we are!" she said as she set the food down in front of Beth and Michiko. "Gregor, this is a little snack for you," she said as she set one of the small plates on his tray. On it was a thinly-sliced strawberry drizzled with a honey-like sauce.

"Hrmph," Gregor said as Mandy left. He took a disdainful sniff. Then, he took a deeper one. Then, he picked up a strawberry slice and nibbled it tentatively. His eyes widened, and his whiskers sprung out. He shoved the slice in his mouth and chewed slowly, eyes half-closed, cheeks bulging.

Michiko had added a small flood of syrup to her pancake stack and was eating happily. Beth had just finished her first bite of her omelet. "My God," she said.

"Something wrong?" Michiko asked.

"No. No, this—this is great. The omelet—the potatoes—"

"You should try the pancakes. Here." Michiko cut out a slice and slipped it onto Beth's plate.

Beth speared the pancake slice and bit it. She smiled as she chewed. "Wow!" she said. "Is there anything here that isn't delicious?"

Michiko thought it over for a moment. "Maybe the napkins?"

Beth giggled and returned to her omelet as Aloysius popped out of the kitchen again. "How's everything?" he asked.

"Yummy!" Michiko said.

"Terrific!" the chef said. "And yours, Beth?"

"Aloysius," she said, "if I were looking and you did dishes and windows, I just might be tempted to ask you out."

"If I were looking and you were a man, I just might listen."

"Figures." Beth smiled.

"I like this one!" Aloysius said to Michiko. "But I have got to tell you about my visitor just now."

"Wrexham's agent?" Michiko asked.

Mandy came over. "Yeah, what did he want?"

Aloysius pulled out a scroll from underneath his apron and unrolled it. "He's throwing a big party tonight."

He set the scroll on the table. Mandy read from it, "'To celebrate the heroic rescue of the storied faerie Puck, and to commemorate his pending return to the Courts of Faerie, our beloved Duke of Wrexham will hold a celebratory gala this evening starting at 5:00 P.M. Guests welcome.'"

"How did you get invited?" Beth asked.

"Oh, I used to work for him," Aloysius said. "I was the chief chef, you could say."

"So why'd you quit?"

"It got boring. He's a seafood fanatic, and it was always twice-baked hagfish this and barnacle souffle that. Oh, and the being a loud spoiled temperamental jerk part."

"That might outweigh the perks," Beth said. "So Puck will be there?"

"That's what the invitation says," Michiko said.

"You know, Michiko…"

"We should crash the party?"

"Exactly! We can snoop around and try to find out what happened to the Professor."

"And maybe get some dirt on Wrexham's plans!" Michiko said. "Good thinking, Beth!"

"Aw, thanks." Beth smiled.

Michiko spun in her seat to face Aloysius. "So, you're taking us?"

He shook his head. "Oh, I'm not going," he said. "The Duke only invited me so he could try to talk me into working for him again. I'm happy here."

"I'd be happy if you'd get back in your kitchen," Mandy said.

"Have the dwarves ordered yet?"

"No. One of them can't decide."

"Clyde can handle things until he does. I don't want any more wasted food today."

"Wasted—" Mandy's eyes lit up. "Is Puck's omelet still there?"

"Under the heat lamp," Aloysius told her. She nodded and headed for the kitchen.

"So how do we get in if you're not going?" Beth asked.

"Simple enough," Aloysius said. "Does anyone have a pen I can borrow?" Michiko pulled one from her pocket and handed it to him. "Thank you," he said as he knelt over the scroll. "How many guests?"

"Three," Michiko said. "We should bring Gregor."

Aloysius nodded and scribbled a quick note on the invitation. Then, he licked his thumb, spoke a few words under his breath, and pressed his wet thumbprint on to the invitation. "Michiko?" he said. She licked her thumb and pressed it next to his print. "Perfect!" he said. "You're all set."

"Thanks!" Michiko said, putting her pen away.

"You're welcome. Just—just find out what happened, okay?" Aloysius asked. "I miss the old Puck." He shook his head.

"Yeah. So do I," Beth said. She stared sadly down at her plate, lost in thoughts and memories.

Michiko reached over and gently squeezed Beth's shoulder. "Me too," she said. "But I'll do what I can to get him back."

Beth looked up at her and smiled. "You mean, we'll do what we can," she said. Michiko returned her smile.

"Hey! Jake and Jake!"

Mandy came out of the kitchen, carrying an omelet split over two plates. It was covered in a red sauce, and it seemed to be not just steaming but smoking as well. "It's your lucky day!" she said as she set the plates down on the Jakes' table. "Can't let this go to waste, so it's yours."

"Really?" Little Jake asked.

Mandy nodded, keeping a straight face. "On the house."

"Hot dang! Free grub!" Little Jake grabbed a fork, Big Jake did the same, and they both scooped up and chewed large bites of omelet.

Their eyes popped open. Their skin turned beet-red. Their eyes watered. Steam seemed to come out of their ears. Big Jake grabbed a full pitcher of water from a nearby table and swallowed the entire contents in two gulps. Little Jake grabbed the glass of ice water from Scylla's table, drank the water, and started gargling with the ice cubes.

"Touche," Beth said with a smile. Aloysius's jaw had dropped. Michiko and Gregor were hysterical with laughter, as were many of the other diners. Even Scylla was smiling.

The dwarves watched with amazement. Finally, one of them cleared his throat and said to Mandy, "I'll have what they're having."

It was late in the morning when Michiko, Beth and Gregor headed out from Wonderland. As they started back down the dirt trail, Beth said, "Michiko?"

"Yessss?"

"Can I come here every Sunday?" Beth asked.

"Maybe," Michiko said. Beth harrumphed in response, and Michiko laughed.

"Serious question," Beth said. "Where is the party, and how do we get there?"

"It's all in the invitation," the Monkey Queen said. "I'll show you back at the apartment."

Chapter Nine

"No!" Beth said. "Not that!"

"It'll be okay," Michiko said. "Just this one time."

"But—but I can't do it. I just can't."

"Let me, then." Michiko reached out.

Beth threw her back against the wall of her apartment. "Not my David Tennant poster!" she cried with mock anguish as she stood in front of it. It was a giant-sized poster, taking up a large part of the wall near the front door.

Michiko sighed. "Beth, that's the only spot here where there's room to put up the invitation. We just need to take the poster down for a while."

"Why not put the invitation on the door?"

"It might cause things to malfunction. That would not be pleasant."

"I'll do it, then," Beth said. She removed the pushpins from the top edge of the poster, carefully rolled it down towards the bottom, then took off the pins there.

"See?" Michiko said. "That wasn't so bad, was it?"

Beth stuck her tongue out at Michiko as she gently set the rolled poster on top of a bookshelf. "So why do we need that much space?" she asked.

"It's for the invitation," Michiko said. "It's actually an artificial, temporary auldgate that leads to the hall where the party is being held. They're called 'porths'."

"How does it work?"

"Faerie magic. At or after the time marked on the invitation, I'll activate the porth. It'll open and expand, and we enter it and walk through a passageway to the party. Then when it's over, we walk back, and the porth closes after we pass through and come home."

"That must create problems if you want to stay over at a friend's place afterward."

"Arrangements can be made." Michiko winked. "And it keeps out party crashers."

"Unless you know someone." Beth grinned.

"Yep!" Michiko sat on the couch and pulled her smartphone from her pocket. "Next, we need fancy outfits, the gaudier the better." She eyed Beth. "We're not the same dress size, are we?"

"Don't worry. I'm covered."

"Huh?"

"Cosplayer," Beth said. "I just have to dig out one of my old costumes and alter it a little. How about you?"

"I just need to make a quick phone call," Michiko said as she tapped the smartphone's screen.

"You know a seamstress?"

"This is quicker. Feng? Hiiii! I need a favor..."

Feng arrived at the apartment twenty minutes later with three boxes and a garment bag for Michiko. By then, Beth was in her bedroom, madly digging through her closet. She found the dress she wanted, tried it on, and then let it out while grumbling. She made a few other alterations before Michiko interrupted her with leftover pizza.

After lunch, Beth followed Michiko's advice and laid down to take a nap. With all that had happened the last two days, she thought sleeping would be impossible, so she was surprised when she woke up two hours later. She took a quick shower, got dressed, and did her hair in a simple updo—the first time in a long time, she realized, that she hadn't just combed her hair and been done with it. A touch of makeup and a pair of heels, and she strode, a bit wobbily, out of the bedroom.

"Michiko?" she asked. "Are you ready—" She saw Michiko and cut her question short.

The Monkey Queen was wearing a floor-length yellow gown, taken in at the waist, with long, puffy sleeves. The embroidered red and dark gold floral pattern was reminiscent of formal Chinese dress, but the petticoats, and the lacy collar and hems, were Western touches. She was wearing short yellow heels, had accessorized with diamond jewelry and a hint of lipstick, and had combed out her hair. "Do I look okay?" she asked, fidgeting nervously.

"Are you kidding?" Beth said. "You look great!"

"Thanks." Michiko blushed and smiled.

"Where did you get that dress?"

"Grandmother Fox had it made for me. We've had to go to some fancy dinners. I had to borrow the jewelry, though. I've got some spares if you need anything." Michiko pointed to a box on the couch.

"Thanks. My jewelry's not fancy enough." Beth dug out a necklace and earrings. "Where's your staff?"

"Somewhere safe." Michiko grinned. "I never thought I'd see you all dressed up! You look wonderful!"

"I'm full of surprises. And thanks." Beth smiled.

"Did you sew that?"

"Every stitch!" Beth said with pride. She was wearing a navy blue, long-sleeved Victorian-style gown that stopped just short of the floor, with black trim that matched her hose and heels and ruffles everywhere. "I made it for a sci-fi convention; it was a steampunk thing. I took off all the mech trimmings a while back, and I just sewed in this lace." She tapped the black lace that covered her collarbone and areas below it.

"Why?"

"I'm not going to have a bunch of faerie perverts looking down my dress. How about Gregor?"

Michiko grinned and gestured towards the cage. Gregor was wearing a mini tuxedo top, cut to fit a guinea pig, with a bow tie. "He's all set!" she said.

"You look…quite formal," Beth said.

"I look like a contestant in a pet show from Hell," Gregor grumbled.

"But a cute one!" Michiko said.

"Let's get this over with," Gregor said. Beth set the purse on the table, and the guinea pig crawled into it. "There had better be strawberries there."

"Beth, before we go," Michiko said, "we need to go over a few things." Beth nodded. "First off, we'll probably be the only humans there. We'll be in for a lot of abuse from some of the guests."

"No surprise there," Beth said.

"Just remember, it's nothing personal. Except against all of humanity."

"Don't slug the obnoxious losers. Got it."

"If you can get into any conversations, do it. See what info we can get."

"What if I run into the Professor?" Beth asked.

Michiko shook her head. "You should stay out of his way."

"But—"

"No buts," Michiko said. "We can't risk getting tossed out for causing a scene."

Beth sighed and nodded. "Anything else?"

"One last thing. If any of the Dukes or anyone in their entourages offer you anything to eat or drink, say 'no', but politely."

"The old 'eat faerie food and you'll be their slave for life' trick?" Beth said.

"Yep! Stick to the buffet tables." Michiko grinned.

"Got it. All set?"

"Are we late now?"

"Only fashionably so." Beth picked up Gregor's purse.

"Wait!" Michiko grabbed her smartphone and stood in front of the invitation, which was pushpinned to the wall where the poster had been. Beth hurried over and stood next to her. They crouched together, smiling, and Michiko held the phone out at arm's length and snapped a selfie.

Michiko set the phone on a bookshelf. Then, she licked her thumb and pressed it against the invitation. As they watched, it darkened, then expanded, flowing out until it covered a large swath of the wall. "Party time!" Michiko said. She took Gregor's purse and held it by the flap; the guinea pig leaned against her fingers. She laid her other hand on Beth's shoulder and guided her into the porth.

Within ten steps of passing through the porth, the light from Beth's apartment had faded, and they were walking through shadow. "Michiko?" Beth asked, trying to keep the worry out of her voice.

"It's okay," Michiko said. "I know it's a bit spooky."

"How do we know where we're going?"

"Look down."

Beth did, and saw a lighted line set in the ground beneath them, reminding her of movie theater floor lights, stretching into the distance. "Got it," she said. "So...fairies use these all the time?"

Michiko shook her head. "It takes a lot of work, and magical energy, to create one porth, never mind dozens. They're usually only created for emergencies or special occasions."

"So, this is basically Wrexham showing off," Beth said. Michiko snickered, and Beth added, "Where does this lead to?"

"I'm sure it won't be Wrexham's estate, but aside from that, I don't know. It could be somewhere else in Faerie, somewhere on Earth, or maybe even somewhere between worlds."

"So try not to use the front door when we leave?"

"Yep!" Michiko said with a grin as they approached a door-shaped light in the darkness.

They emerged from the porth onto a sprawling landing. The staircase it topped was wide enough to hold a herd of elephants, with room left over for a hippo or two. The stairs led down to a ballroom that could have doubled as a convention center, or a football field. Hundreds of faeries were already mingling, talking loudly, and getting lost. A small orchestra tried to make themselves heard on a stage against the far wall.

"Time to make an entrance!" Michiko said, nodding to an elderly faerie in full butler regalia standing stiffly nearby. He presented a blank piece of well-worn paper to her; she licked her thumb and pressed it on the paper.

He held up the paper and read, "Announcing Aloysius Alphonsus!" The partygoers nearest the stairs paused and looked up at him; he continued, "He sends greetings, but he is unable to attend, for he fears he is coming down with the vapors. In his place, he presents the Monkey Queen and two companions."

Michiko and Beth descended the stairs, smiling and waving like beauty pageant contestants. "I should have brought my smartphone!" Beth whispered.

"It wouldn't have worked here anyway," Michiko whispered back. "Wrexham is a total Luddite." Beth giggled.

They walked past two overdressed faerie women who turned up their noses as they passed. "Humans," one said.

"So immature," said the other.

"And what horrible attire!"

"So common."

"I must admit, though—I like the purse." The other one nodded.

Michiko was all smiles as she weaved through the crowd. Beth stayed close as she tried to copy Michiko's example, but she found it difficult. She was both fascinated and overwhelmed by what she was seeing.

Most of the attendees were faeries, and almost all of them had gotten decked out. The men wore silken robes or tunics over leggings, and the women wore dresses of the finest fabric, all in the colors of their houses. Their hair was perfect without exception, and their jewelry would have made Liz Taylor weep with envy. They all moved with well-practiced and premeditated grace. Their speech was cordial and thoroughly pre-rehearsed. And their glares and sneers cut through Beth like the sharpest needles.

The hall had plenty of alcoves and quiet corners along the walls, presumably for discussions of a private or sensitive nature. Michiko led Beth into one, asking, "So what do you think?"

"It's like all the cheerleaders and jocks in high school got together to pick on me," Beth said, "but on a much grander scale."

"Ignore them," Michiko said as she opened Beth's purse. "Gregor?"

The guinea pig stuck his head out. "Strawberry time?"

"Strawberries later. Eavesdropping now." She pulled Gregor out. "Sweep the room. Try to avoid being seen. Listen in on anything you can involving Puck or Wrexham. If it's anything important, find me or Beth ASAP."

"Is there anything else?"

"Yes. Try not to get stepped on." Michiko set Gregor on the floor.

"Oh, thank you so very much," Gregor said as he scurried off.

Michiko turned back to Beth. "You too, Beth. See if you can find anyone here who's willing to talk. And avoid Puck."

"And don't get stepped on," Beth said with a sigh.

Michiko grinned and left the alcove, ducking past a waiter. Beth waited a minute, then swallowed hard and moved into the crowd.

Michiko watched as the faerie servant walked past, doing his studied best not to notice her. She took advantage of that to slip a glass off the tray he carried. She sniffed its contents, made a face, and emptied it into a nearby potted plant.

"Monkey Queen!"

She turned and saw Duke Wrexham approach her, fake smile in place, trailed by two of his men. "What a surprise to see you here!" he said.

"Slow TV night," she said. "But—"

"Oh, look!" Wrexham said. "Your glass is empty! Men, get that special bottle from my…private stock."

"You know, I'm not old enough for that," Michiko said. The duke ignored her.

The other faeries nodded and hurried off. As soon as they were gone, Wrexham dropped the facade. "Why are you here?" he said.

"I missed you!" she said with a grin. "It's been hours!"

"Don't play games with me, Monkey Queen! Who sent you?"

"Your former chef. I need to steal some recipes."

Wrexham's eyes narrowed. "You're here about Puck, aren't you?"

"He's no chef."

"I should throw you out of here right now!"

"And create a scene in the middle of your big bash?" Michiko said, her grin widening.

Wrexham suddenly smiled again, as his men returned with a small bottle. "Ah, I see! Well, Monkey Queen, you're welcome here. Enjoy yourself! Stay for the entertainment! In fact—" He uncorked the bottle. "Would you care to join me in a toast, with my compliments?"

Michiko laughed and shook her head. "I never drink and walk through porths." She spun away from Wrexham and back into the crowd; he scowled as he re-corked the bottle.

When Beth was younger and had seen too many movies with princesses, she had occasionally dreamed about great parties, glorious balls with hundreds of attendees. And she would show up at the ball, be herself, and win everyone over with her charm and wit.

So much for that daydream, Beth thought as she stood in a darkened alcove. The party-goers had ignored her when she tried talking to them, and she had heard some of them snickering as she walked away. Try as she might to keep up her spirits, she was beginning to feel depressed and alone, the way she always felt at parties. She sighed and steeled herself for a trip across the floor, figuring that even if the rest of the party stunk, the buffet tables would be interesting.

"Beth McGill."

The voice chilled Beth to the bone. She turned around.

There was a woman in the shadows. They drifted and wove around her, they blended into her hair and trailed from her black clothing. All Beth could see clearly of her were her dark eyes. "Who are you?" Beth asked. "How did you get in here?"

"Faerie porths go through shadows," the woman said, "as do I."

"Okay. How did you know my name?"

"So many questions." The woman smiled. "And I have some for you."

"Huh?"

"The Monkey Queen. Do you trust her?"

"That's none of your—"

"What if I were to tell you that she was wrong?"

"About what?" Beth said. "She's been right about everything so far."

"But she won't always be. What will you do when that time comes?" the woman said, a hint of menace in her voice. "When the future stretches before you, what side will you be on? What will you choose?"

Beth said nothing. She stared into the shadows and blinked.

"Clever girl!" the woman said. "Perhaps we should continue this discussion elsewhere." She raised a shadow-wrapped arm.

Beth backed away. "No, thanks," she said. "I prefer a little less vagueness in my conversations."

The woman nodded. "Very well then. Just don't expect such kindness from me the next time we meet."

"The next—" Beth started to say, but the woman took a step back, into the shadows. They wrapped around her, they swallowed her, and they vanished.

Beth blinked and shook her head. "Was she threatening me?" she said to herself. In a bit of a daze, she turned and stepped out of the alcove. As she did, a quartet of young, swaggering faeries wearing Wrexham's colors walked by. One of them stuck out his foot, tripping Beth.

Her knees hit the floor first, then her hands as she used them to break her fall. She grimaced, but managed not to shout as pain flooded her body. She caught her breath, grateful that nothing had broken and her glasses had stayed on. Then, she could hear the faeries laughing at her. "Clumsy!" the one who tripped her said with a mocking smile. "Just what you'd expect from a human." They walked away, their laughter growing.

Beth slowly got to her knees. They were sore, as were the heels of her hands, and her face was burning with embarrassment. *Maybe I am in over my head*, she thought. *Maybe Puck was—*

"Are you all right?"

Beth looked and saw a faerie bending down, extending a hand to her. She was wearing a green tunic over matching leggings and a mail coat, sword at her side. On the front of the tunic was an emblem displaying a crossed sword and leaf. She had long curly blond hair, and her eyes were dark and deep enough to remind Beth of Puck. "I'll be okay, thanks," Beth said as the faerie helped her up.

"I am sorry," the faerie said. "We're not all like that. I hope you'll remember that."

"I will."

The faerie nodded. "Excuse me," she said, and she was gone, lost in the crowd before Beth could say another word.

Figures, Beth thought. *First friendly person here who talks to me, and she's with security or something.* Shaking her head again, she set off for the buffet tables.

Michiko was near the stage, watching the orchestra, as Duke Wrexham approached her again. "Monkey Queen!" he said with a phony laugh.

"Nice band you have here," she said. "Do they take requests?"

Wrexham blinked. "Pardon?"

"You know, like Mozart? The Beatles? 'Gangnam Style'?"

"Oh. Earth music. How droll," the Duke said. "No, I have something for you."

Michiko raised an eyebrow. "I thought you were married."

"I thought you might be hungry by now," he said, "so I brought this for you." One of his men came up carrying a dessert plate with a domed glass cover; Wrexham removed the cover with a flourish.

On the dish was a plain pound cake, topped with chopped walnuts and dusted with powdered sugar. The cake had a pleasant, earthly smell to it that caught the attention of nearby faeries. "It's fresh from my kitchens," Wrexham said. "You must try it, with my compliments. I insist."

Michiko giggled. "Oh, I'm afraid I couldn't!" she said, looking back as she slipped into the crowd. "I have to watch my girlish figure, you know!" Wrexham snarled wordlessly as he slapped the cover back on the dish.

Beth finally allowed herself a smile as she reached the buffet tables. Even though most of the guests seemed not to be eating, as long as no one else was looking, she was hungry. She grabbed a small plate and eyed the food.

It seemed to be standard high-class party fare, at least as prepared faerie style. One small table was loaded with seafood, including a plate with something that looked like a sugar-coated gray ball. She reached for one of the balls.

"I'd recommend against that."

Beth drew her hand back and glanced at the speaker. He was tall, chubby and reptilian, with smooth green and purple skin, a long tail and thick arms and legs. He wore a black robe with red and gold stitching, oversized glasses with round lenses, and a red hat that looked like someone had stolen the tassel off a giant fez.

Two days ago, Beth thought, *I would have fled the room screaming at the sight of him.* "Why?" she asked. "What's wrong with it?"

"It's no so much that anything's 'wrong'," the reptile said. "It's just that some of the ingredients in there might severely upset the human digestive system."

"What is it, anyway? A dessert?"

"Crystallized jellied eel, actually."

"And the tray next to it?" Beth pointed at a pile of something green and rounded.

"Pickled sea slug."

Beth tried not to gag. "Thanks."

"You're welcome. Try the sausage in pastry on the next table; I hear it's quite good." Beth did so as the reptile grabbed a slug from the tray and popped it in his mouth. "Not bad," he said, "but I miss Wrexham's old chef. Now there was someone who knew how to pickle a sea slug."

"You're right about the sausage," Beth said. She loaded several more on her plate, then added some carrot sticks and celery out of guilt. "Try one?"

"Thank you, but pork affects me much the same as the seafood here would affect you."

Beth nodded. "I'm Beth McGill, by the way."

"I am called Olig." He wiped his hand on a napkin and extended it towards Beth. "What do you do, Beth?"

She shook his hand. "I'm an English major in college, when I'm not eavesdropping at parties."

"You came in with the Monkey Queen?"

"You've heard of her?" Beth raised an eyebrow.

Olig nodded. "She's getting quite the reputation in Faerie. Some of my clients speak of her. Usually while gritting their teeth or cursing."

"That sounds like her. How's the punch?"

"Safe to drink, not spiked, and quite tasty." Olig held out a glass. "Would you be so kind?"

"Sure." Beth ladled punch in his glass, then her own, then took a sip. "So, Olig, what do you do?"

"I'm an interdimensional facilitator."

"What does that mean?"

"I take people between worlds. No auldgates or porths needed."

"Really!" Beth said with an excited smile.

Olig nodded. "You'd be surprised how many faerie nobles will sneak off for a vacation on Earth. Not that I can name names."

"Like the Duke?"

"Well…" Olig pondered. "He's been spending a lot of time on Earth."

"I know." Beth made a face.

"You've met him, I take it."

"You know him?"

Olig shrugged. "He pays well. He was acting a bit odd last week, though. First, he summoned me to Earth, and then had me take him and his entourage back to Faerie."

"To his Court?" Beth asked.

"No. To the edge of the forest, near the Hoblands."

"Why there?"

"He didn't say. I suspect a summer cottage may be involved."

Beth suspected otherwise, and decided that it was time to change the subject. "So, how does one get a job as an interdimensional facilitator?"

"One has to be born for it. It's an incredibly rare talent. I found out I had it when I was four."

"What happened?"

Olig blushed slightly. "My mother took away my favorite toy after I misbehaved. I threw quite the temper tantrum, yelling that I was going away. To my surprise, I did."

"Where to?"

"Somewhere far, far away. All I remember is that it was dark and cold and empty." Olig seemed to shudder at the memory. "I cried because I wanted to go home, and I pictured my house and my family and wished real hard, and suddenly I was back."

"Were your parents mad?" Beth asked.

"Remarkably, no. They were just as scared as I was! As soon as I returned, they took me to a neighborhood wizard who figured out what happened."

"So what did he do?"

"He put a restraining spell on me to make sure that it didn't happen again. He said my parents were having enough headaches as it was." Olig grinned.

Beth laughed. "But they finally took the spell off, obviously."

"Only when I was old enough to get the training to control my trips. And I've been doing this ever since."

"Is it just from Earth to Faerie and back?"

"Oh, my stars, no! I'm not even from either of those places. My homeworld is called Fip."

"Fip?"

"It's a wonderful place." Beth could hear the pride in Olig's voice. "You should see it in the fall, when the firebats' annual migration lights up the night sky."

"Maybe someday. If I survive this party."

"I know the feeling. But I do need to start mingling again. Drumming up business."

Beth nodded. "It was nice meeting you, Olig."

"Likewise. But before I go—" He reached inside his robe and pulled out a card. "Take this, in case the Monkey Queen, or you, ever need to get somewhere. The instructions are on the back."

Beth took the card. "Thanks," she said with a smile.

"You're welcome. Just remember that you can always use it to go see the firebats."

"I just may."

Olig returned Beth's smile and waved as he walked away. *Time to find Michiko,* she thought. She gathered some strawberries for Gregor, wrapped them in a napkin and put them in her purse; Olig's card went in as well, in a side pocket. Then, she gave in to temptation and grabbed one last sausage.

"Clumsy idiot!" Gregor grumbled as he dodged another pair of faerie high heels. He had been spending most of his time at the party trying to not get stepped on, and the rest trying to get on the buffet tables. He had so far succeeded at the first and failed at the second.

He moved along the wall, considering what to do next, when four young faeries in red and gold walked past, talking boastfully and laughing loudly. One of them then turned his head towards the guinea pig.

Gregor darted away, running under the curtain that covered one alcove. "Was that a rat I just saw?" the faerie shouted.

"That ugly human you tripped must have brought it in!" another one said, bringing out more laughter from his companions.

"If this place wasn't so crowded," Gregor muttered, "I'd teach those punks—"

He stopped when he realized who else was in the alcove. Lord Wrexham stood next to Puck, who was now dressed in Wrexham's colors. They were talking to a faerie woman in green with curly blonde hair who wore a sword. Gregor scampered into a corner and listened.

"Duke Wrexham, I plead with you!" the woman was saying. "This is madness! First the spriggans, now this!"

"What gives you the right to question me?" he said, his voice cold.

"I've been out there," she said. "I've actually spent time there. They're not perfect, we all know. But they're trying!"

"It's not enough."

"Or is it just what their land has to offer now? Is it your greed, and not the good of Faerie—"

"Stand down!" the Duke said.

The woman turned towards Puck. "Godfather—Puck! Are you supporting this?"

He nodded. "The Duke is doing the right thing for Faerie."

"But it's not right! You know that!" Her voice softened. "What has happened to you?"

"People change," Puck said.

Wrexham put an arm around Puck's shoulders. "My decision was and is final. Your duty is to accept it and obey your lord."

"You are not my lord," the woman spat out. "I have no lord here." She threw the curtain aside and stormed out.

Wrexham and Puck faced each other and spoke, too softly for Gregor to hear. He dashed out of the alcove, looking for Michiko and Beth.

The faerie servant tried not to sweat as he carried the glass-domed tray that held four chocolate chip cookies up to the human. "M-M-Monkey Queen?" he said.

"Yessss?" Michiko said.

"L-L-Lord Wrexham presents this to you, with his compliments." Hands shaking, the servant held out the tray.

"For me? Thanks!"

The servant started to sigh with relief, but then gasped as Michiko took the tray from him, cookies and all. "But—" he tried to say.

"It's perfect! It'll look so nice in my dining nook!" She spun away from the servant and walked off before he could say another word.

As Michiko worked her way through the crowd, she saw a group of four young faeries in red and gold near her, passing an all-but-empty bottle between them. "Oh, look!" one of them said. "Another human!"

"She's almost as horrid as that clumsy one!" another faerie said, triggering a round of drunken laughter.

As it died down, Michiko grinned and took the lid off the tray. "I can't be that bad!" she said. "I have cookies for you, after all."

"Cookies?"

"Compliments of the Monkey Queen!"

The faerie took a cookie from the tray and bit into it. His face lit up. The others each grabbed one and dug in. "Enjoy!" Michiko said as she walked off.

"Monkey Queen?"

Michiko turned and saw Vrech and Amitya standing off to the side, both wearing formal red and black outfits and looking very uncomfortable. "Hiiii!" she said with a smile. "Surprised to see me here?"

"I am," Vrech said, "but I shouldn't be, should I?"

"I'm at all the big parties!" Michiko's smile vanished. "You were invited? I'm surprised you showed up."

Amitya sighed. "We considered not going, but we felt that Wrexham would be offended by the snub."

"Faerie politics," Vrech said. "Have you heard anything?"

"Not yet," Michiko said, "but I need to check with Beth and Gregor. And find a place to stash this tray." She set off into the crowd.

Beth stood by the buffet tables and scowled. She had been circling the room looking for Michiko for what seemed like an eternity, but hadn't seen her, and now her feet were hurting. She reached for a cup and the punch ladle.

"Beth!" Michiko shouted from behind her.

"Oh, now you show up," Beth said as she turned around.

"Sorry. Wrexham keeps trying to tempt me. How's the food that's safe to eat?"

"Try the sausage, skip the sea slug. Find anything out?"

"Vrech and Amitya are here." Michiko grabbed a handful of carrot sticks.

"They were invited?" Beth raised an eyebrow.

"Yep," Michiko said as she munched. "That tells me that Wrexham is up to something."

"He must be. I was talking to this guy I met—"

"You met a guy?" Michiko said, smiling slyly. "Did you give him your phone number?"

Beth rolled her eyes. "He's an interdimensional facilitator, and he's not even my species. He's green and purple. And reptilian."

"You were flirting with Barney the Dinosaur?"

"Michiko…"

"Okay, okay! What did he have to tell you?"

"He said that he had taken Wrexham and some of his men to a spot near the Hoblands a few days ago. He didn't know why Wrexham would want to go there."

Michiko nodded. "There's something not right—"

"Girl! Down here!"

Michiko and Beth looked down and saw Gregor. "Enjoying the party?" Michiko asked.

"Not in the slightest," the guinea pig said. "But I do have a story to tell."

Beth lifted Gregor up, and he told the women what he had heard. By the time he had finished, Michiko was scowling. "That cinches it," she said. "Wrexham's up to no good."

Beth opened up her purse. "Nice work, Gregor," she said. "I got you a snack." She slipped the guinea pig into the purse; he squealed happily.

"It's coming together," Michiko said. "But how does Puck fit in? What is Wrexham up to?"

"I think we're about to find out." Beth grabbed Michiko and pointed to the stage. The orchestra had stopped, and Cantwick was trying to get the crowd's attention. As he started to speak, Beth noticed something odd about him, something she couldn't quite put a finger on. She looked past the surface and saw that the faerie had covered his face with a seeming. Below it, his right eye was bruised. *Was he in a fight?* she thought. *Or did he just get a little too fresh with someone?*

"Hear ye, hear ye!" Cantwick shouted. "We are pleased and honored to present to you our majestic and beloved lord, the Duke of Wrexham!" The faeries applauded politely. Beth bit her lip.

The Duke smiled and waved as he stepped on the stage. Puck followed him, copying his smile. "Ladies and gentlemen of Faerie!" the Duke said to the crowd. "I thank you all for coming on such short notice. As you can see, I have good news: we have rescued Puck from the clutches of his kidnappers and returned him to our homelands!" Puck nodded as most of the crowd applauded again. Beth stopped biting her lip; she was worried about chomping through it.

"Even though he is safe and sound," the Duke said, "there is still the matter of dealing with those who committed this heinous crime. Puck has told us that it was done by the hobgoblins." Beth glanced around the crowd and saw Vrech clenching his fists.

"Too long have they defied and denied us! Too long have we allowed this to continue! Well, no longer!" Wrexham thundered. "We will have our vengeance! I am pleased to announce that as of now, the House of Wrexham declares war upon the Hoblands!"

The crowd applauded, with more enthusiasm than before. As Wrexham continued his speech, Michiko said to Beth, "There's one piece in place. This is all a set-up for Wrexham to get what he wants. But where does Puck—"

"Michiko?" Beth said. "We've got a more immediate problem." She pointed back to the stage.

"Two of the hobgoblins who were behind this," Wrexham was saying, "are in this hall tonight! We shall make them pay for their crime!" He stepped off the stage to another round of applause.

"That's no way to treat invited guests!" Michiko said.

"I know," Beth said, glancing at a nearby trio of faerie guards. "But how do we stop him?"

"Monkey Queen?"

Michiko turned and saw the four faeries who she had given the cookies to earlier. They were staring at her, expressionless and glassy-eyed. "My liege," said one in a hollow voice, "we are in your service. What would you have us do?"

"I have just the thing," Michiko said, grinning.

Vrech glared at Duke Wrexham as the faerie approached him and Amitya. "This is an outrage!" the hobgoblin shouted. "We had nothing to do with Puck's abduction! You know it!"

"But you can't prove that." The Duke smiled cruelly. "I believe you were in on the plot all along. The ringleader, in fact."

"What?" Vrech said, visibly shocked.

"How dare you!" Amitya said.

"This is my realm," Wrexham said, "and my word is law. Guards?" He gestured. Three faerie guards on the far side of the room drew their swords and started towards Vrech and Amitya.

"Conga line!" someone shouted.

Heads throughout the room turned. Four young faeries wearing Wrexham's colors had formed a line and were dancing through the crowd. They marched between the hobgoblins and Wrexham, who had to dodge their poorly-synchronized kicks. "Celebrate our glorious declaration of war by joining in the conga line and dancing, as my liege commands!" the lead faerie loudly declared.

With squeals of delight, other faeries jumped into the line. The conductor shrugged and led the orchestra in a vamp that managed to sound nothing like conga music. The quickly-growing line cut off the guards, keeping them away from the hobgoblins. "What is this?" Vrech asked. "What is going on?"

"It's called a distraction," Beth said as she popped up next to him. "The Monkey Queen says it's a good time to get out." Vrech nodded, took Amitya's arm and headed towards the stairs, Beth trailing behind.

"Stop them!" Wrexham shouted, trying to be heard above the orchestra and the call to conga. Two guards near the stairs started to move, but the hobgoblins were already past the greeter, and into the porth.

The line grew longer, snaking around the room. The orchestra did its best to keep up. Wrexham glanced around, befuddled. "Who—?" he started to ask.

"Not in the mood for conga, Duke?"

He turned towards Michiko as she pushed something into his hands. "You can have it back," she said. "It doesn't match my tea caddy."

Wrexham looked down at his dessert tray and saw the few crumbs remaining there. He looked at the conga line and saw the glazed expressions of its four leaders. He saw the Monkey Queen somersaulting over the dancers. "Great party!" she shouted over her shoulder as she landed and headed for the stairs.

"I'll get you!" the Duke screamed. He started to push through the crowd, but as he did, a large figure blocked his way.

"Duke Wrexham!" Olig said with a smile, spreading his arms wide. "Wonderful party as always! The pickled sea slug was excellent...I'm sorry, is this a bad time?"

Wrexham pushed past him without a word, but Michiko and Beth were already on the stairs. He snarled and turned away, handing the dessert tray to the faerie leading the conga line. Behind him, Olig waved at Beth, who smiled and gave a thumbs-up in return. Michiko grabbed Beth's shoulder and slipped a hand into Gregor's purse. They hurried into the porth.

A minute later, as Wrexham's men tried to restore order, a blonde faerie guard in green slipped through the crowd and up the stairs. She looked about, laid a hand on her sword, and with a nod to the greeter, stepped into the porth.

Chapter Ten

"There we are!" Michiko said as she pointed to the lightpath at their feet. "Follow this, and we'll be home."

They started down the lightpath, but Beth found herself shivering. "Something's wrong," she said.

"Don't tell me you tried the pickled sea slug!" Michiko said.

"I think the girl's right," Gregor said. "There's a different...feel to the air."

Michiko nodded. "Let's play it safe and—"

She was cut short by a loud shriek. In the glow of the lightpath, they could see a large, hideous black bird flying towards them. Its eyes glowed red, and it seemed to trail shadow behind it. Beth realized that it could be a twin of the bird that had been at her window two nights before, and tried not to shudder.

Michiko shook her arm, and her miniaturized staff slid out of her sleeve. In an instant, it was its normal size and in her hand. She swung it at the bird as it approached her.

It reared up, then swooped down. Michiko lashed out, striking the bird hard with the staff's tip. The bird seemed to evaporate, fading into the shadows. "We're being attacked," she said. "Gregor, stay down; that bird looked hungry." The guinea pig grumbled but dropped down inside his purse.

"Wrexham?" Beth asked.

"This isn't his style," Michiko said. "But who—"

"Monkey Queen!"

A faerie woman with long blonde hair was running down the lightpath towards them, sword drawn. *Isn't she the woman who—?* Beth thought. Michiko raised her staff.

"Behind you!" the faerie shouted. Michiko turned as the faerie's sword swung past her. The black bird she hit dissipated. "Shadow rooks," she said. "I think more are coming."

"Let's not wait for them," Michiko said. "We don't have too far to go."

"Protect your friend." The faerie moved next to Beth, her back to Michiko. "Move down the lightpath, but not too fast or slow."

Michiko nodded and stepped warily along the path. Beth stayed close to her. The faerie kept right behind Beth; a quick swing of her sword, and another bird vanished.

Then, the air filled with shrieks as a half-dozen more shadow rooks dove from the darkness. Michiko and the faerie both swung, but the birds swooped away and then dove again, talons extended. Michiko pushed Beth aside as two rooks just missed them both. "We're outnumbered," the faerie said as she drove the birds back.

"Cover Beth," Michiko said. She crouched down, then jumped twelve feet in the air.

The shadow rooks converged on the Monkey Queen. She held her staff in one hand and swung widely. Three birds vanished into smoke. She then tossed the staff at two birds attacking the faerie. It hit them both, dissipating them, and clattered to the floor.

As it did, Michiko rebounded off the passageway's wall. As she tumbled back and down, two swift hard kicks and an elbow jab took out three more rooks. She landed on her feet and held out her hand. Her staff flew into it, and she spun and struck two last birds. "I've cleared the path," she said, catching her breath. "Run for it."

Michiko and Beth ran as fast they could in their heels. The faerie followed close behind, swinging her sword as more birds flew after them. "How can she fight like that while wearing that outfit?" she muttered.

They reached the porth and Beth, legs and feet aching, dove through first, tumbling onto the floor of her living room. Michiko was next, spinning back to face the porth as soon as she was through.

The faerie was last, and as she entered the room, she turned and stabbed into the porth, dispatching one last rook. Then, one more slash; the porth vanished, and the two pieces of Aloysius's invitation fluttered to the floor. "Are you all right?" she asked.

"You bet!" Michiko said. "What a party!"

"Yeah, my favorite parties always end up with me running for my life," Beth said as Michiko helped her up. She looked at the faerie, who was sheathing her sword. "You're the one who helped me up when I was tripped, aren't you?" she asked.

The faerie nodded. "I'm sorry I came across so curt before," she said. "I had important business I needed to get to. My name is Robyn. I'm with the Faerie Forest Guard."

"Beth McGill. Thanks for the help back there." They shook hands. "And that's the Monkey Queen."

"My friends call me Michiko," she said as she shook Robyn's hand. Then, her eyes widened. "Wait...I think I've heard of you. Aren't you Puck's goddaughter?"

"That's the human term, yes," the faerie said.

"Oh my gosh!" Michiko smiled. "I'm so glad to meet you! Puck talks about you all the time!"

"I hope he hasn't bored you." Robyn returned Michiko's smile.

There was a muffled, cranky voice from Beth's purse. "This is Gregor," she said, lifting the guinea pig out.

"You use that as a pet carrier?" Robyn said.

"I know!" Gregor grumbled. "It's cruelty to animals."

Robyn raised an eyebrow. "Ventriloquism?"

"Reincarnation," Beth said as she put Gregor in his cage.

"Ah."

"So why are you here?"

"Did they run out of sausages?" Michiko asked.

Robyn blinked. "Actually, I came to ask you for your help."

"With those birds?"

"I think I may have an idea about who's behind that," Beth said. "I spoke to a woman at the party who seemed to be a sorceress. She was doing tricks with shadows. She tried to convince me that Michiko was bad news, then she vanished."

"How did she get in without an invitation?" Robyn asked.

"She mentioned something about going where there were shadows, including faerie porths."

"So we have another crisis?" Gregor asked.

"Tell her to take a number," Michiko said. "We still have to stop a war and find out what happened to Puck."

"Which brings me to why I'm here," Robyn said. "I heard what Wrexham's plans are."

"Conquer the hobgoblins and seize their land?" Michiko said.

"More than that. Right outside the Hoblands, there's an auldgate to Earth that's been closed for centuries."

"Right. It happened during the last True Millennium."

"And we know where the other end is," Beth said. "It's nearby."

"Wrexham is going to reopen that auldgate," Robyn said. "He plans on doing it this morning, and he has 300 soldiers ready, hiding here on Earth."

Beth scowled. "Is reopening it possible?"

"With the True Millennium coming again," Michiko said, "any auldgate that was shut down last time is fair game."

"With it reopened," Robyn said, "he can march in to the Hoblands and catch the hobgoblins by surprise. It will be a slaughter."

"But that's not the only reason you're here, is it, girl?" Gregor said. "You had business with Wrexham and Puck, didn't you?"

The faerie blinked. "How—how did—?"

"When you're small, you can go places you're not supposed to be."

Robyn nodded. "I came because of Puck. He's told me about Earth, and he's mentioned you, Michiko. I thought you might know what happened to him, why he had changed after his kidnapping."

"He's not himself," Beth said. "It's like he's been a different person since he was rescued."

"It's all connected, isn't it?" Michiko said.

"What is?" Robyn asked.

"The kidnapping and Wrexham's declaration of war. I can't figure out how, but they are, and not in the obvious way."

"And the hobgoblins?"

"I'm convinced that Wrexham set them up. But again, I don't know how." Michiko started to pace around the living room.

"That reminds me of something," Beth said. "Michiko, both times that you fought the hobgoblins, there was something odd about them."

"How so?"

"When I blinked, and disrupted their seemings, the hobgoblins still seemed…fuzzy to me. Blurry."

"She has second sight," Michiko said to Robyn. The faerie raised an eyebrow and nodded. "I didn't notice anything, Beth."

"Robyn?" Beth asked. "Do you have a seeming?"

"I have a human one," she said, "but I don't use it much." She gestured, and suddenly she was a blonde human female in green workout clothes and running shoes.

"Gregor?" Beth said. "Can you cast seemings? Temporary ones?"

"Can I cast temporary seemings?" The guinea pig snorted. "Child's play."

"Would you cast one on Robyn?" Beth asked. "On top of her other seeming?" Gregor nodded and spoke quickly under his breath. Robyn became a brunette in a green floor-length dress.

Beth stared at Robyn, looked past the surface but not too far, and blinked. Gregor's seeming vanished, leaving Robyn in her blonde human seeming. "Okay," Beth said. "None of you can see this, but right now, Robyn's seeming is fuzzy."

"So that means…" Michiko said.

"That the kidnappers and the fake cops at the alley weren't hobgoblins," Beth said as Robyn dispelled her seeming. "They had a second seeming that I didn't catch."

"But who were they?"

Beth's eyes widened. "Michiko! At the party! Remember Cantwick? Wrexham's right-hand faerie? He had a black eye!"

"I didn't see anything," Michiko said as she paced.

"He was covering his face with a seeming," Beth said

"Faeries do that all the time."

"But when you fought the hobgoblins, didn't you hit one—"

"But that means—" Michiko started to say as she stopped next to Beth.

"And he was behind it—" Beth said.

"And Puck hasn't been himself—"

"Because he wasn't—"

"And his breakfast!"

"And you told me—"

"And that's why he didn't—"

"Michiko!" Beth said with an excited smile. "Are you pondering what I'm pondering!"

"Yes, I am!" Michiko yelled. They fell into each other's arms, laughing loud and long.

Michiko pulled back. "I need to change," she said. "It's too early to be so dressed up!"

"Same here," Beth said. "These heels are killing me."

"I need to use your kitchen, too."

"Go right ahead."

"But do you have—"

"Lots. The roommate before last had to leave in a hurry."

"Yay!" Michiko bounded into the empty bedroom.

"Don't worry," Beth said, grabbing Robyn's shoulders. "We know what Wrexham is up to. We're going to stop him. And Puck is going to be fine. Count on it."

She ran into her bedroom and shut the door. Robyn stared after her for a long moment. "They're both completely and utterly mad, aren't they?" the faerie finally said.

Gregor snorted. "I could have told you that the moment I saw the bunny slippers."

Michiko had changed into her yellow, black and red outfit and was finishing up in the kitchen. Beth was back in her faded jeans and her green army jacket, under which she was wearing, she hoped ironically, a *Les Miserables* t-shirt. "All set?" she asked the others as she grabbed Gregor's purse. She pulled Olig's card from it and stuck it on a shelf, not expecting to use it but not wanting to lose it.

"Yep!" Michiko slipped something into her pocket and grabbed her staff.

Robyn stood up and loosened her sword in its scabbard. "Aye," she said.

"Have fun out there," Gregor said as he burrowed into his bedding. "Good night."

"Not so fast." Beth scooped the guinea pig from his cage and into his gaudy purse.

As they left Beth's apartment, Michiko pulled out her smartphone and made a call. "Good morning!" she said. "I know it's early, but we need your help. Oh, you can catch up on your beauty sleep later. Listen, you need to call some of the regulars. Tell them to get over to Paulsen Plaza ASAP. That means you, too. You can go back to bed after we prevent a war."

Paulsen Plaza was a small square in the center of town, with trees, bushes, benches, a statue of a forgotten politician, and too many pigeons. It was a dark, chilly, foggy early morning, and several faerie soldiers near the statue were shivering and trying to keep warm. Duke Wrexham was not; he walked briskly up to them. "How is the ritual proceeding, Cantwick?" he asked his right-hand man.

"Slowly but steadily," he said. "The wizards have asked not to be disturbed; any interruption at this point would force them to start over."

"Make sure they are left alone, then. The seemings are holding?"

"Aye. The wizards reassure me that humans will not interfere with us."

"Are the men in place?"

Cantwick nodded. "At your command, as always."

"And Puck?"

"Right here, my liege." Puck walked up to Wrexham and clasped his hand. "A grand day dawns for Faerie, eh?"

"Absolutely." Wrexham smiled. "Cantwick, gather the—"

"Good morning!" Michiko strolled into the plaza, Beth close behind.

"The Monkey Queen." Wrexham sighed. "Of course."

"And good morning, Puck!" Beth said. He ignored her.

"So!" Wrexham said, rubbing his hands. "Come to witness my impending triumph?"

"You're almost finished with the Sunday crossword?" Michiko said.

"So you actually came to mock me. As usual."

"No," Beth said. "We're here to accuse you of framing the hobgoblins for Puck's kidnapping as a pretense for invading the Hoblands."

Wrexham laughed. "Ah, Monkey Queen, your friend is so amusing. Don't you think so, Puck?"

"She always seemed quite mad to me, my liege," Puck said with a sneer.

"Not this time," Beth said. "Michiko?"

Michiko nodded. "To begin with, Duke, your house has coveted the Hoblands for decades, right? Ever since the Uprising?"

"I have honored the Compact," Wrexham said. "The hobgoblins chose not to."

"Robyn?"

The faerie emerged from behind a tree. "With all due respect, Duke," she said, "I have spent a great deal of time recently in the Forest Guard near the Hoblands, observing the hobgoblins. They have not violated the Compact."

"Except in the matter of my kidnapping!" Puck shouted. "Which Duke Wrexham rescued me from!"

"A rescue that no one witnessed," Beth said, "and that no one knew about until you two showed up after we visited the hobgoblin warehouse nearby. Which was after we had to break through a barrier spell, which the hobgoblins couldn't have created, to find evidence that was planted there."

"And I would have walked right into that barrier," Michiko said, "if Beth hadn't seen something there."

"Which means that the barrier wasn't a safeguard," Beth said. "It was a trap for the Monkey Queen."

"Which reminds me," Michiko said. "I fought several hobgoblins in front of that alley. During the fight, I hit one of them on the right side of his face."

"I had disrupted their seemings earlier," Beth said, "but they still looked fuzzy to me. I didn't realize it at the time, but they had overlaid one seeming on top of another."

"And Beth noticed something odd at the party," Michiko said. "Cantwick had a seeming covering his face. Why would he need one?"

Beth picked up on her cue. She glanced at Cantwick, looked beneath the surface and blinked. "That's why," she said as the seeming vanished, revealing Cantwick's black eye.

"So, Cantwick," Michiko asked, "where did you get that shiner?" The faerie reflexively covered his right eye. "From fighting me," she said, "while you and the others were disguised as hobgoblins. Just like the faeries who kidnapped Puck."

"And there's your conclusion," Beth said. "Duke Wrexham was behind Puck's kidnapping, and set things up to pin the blame on the hobgoblins. He was going to use it as justification to attack the Hoblands, and to get his revenge on Puck."

"I've had enough of this nonsense and supposition!" Duke Wrexham said, folding his arms. "Guards!"

"No." All eyes turned to Robyn. "As a captain of the Forest Guard, and acting with legal authority, I am ordering you to stop, Duke. Please continue, Monkey Queen."

"Thank you!" Michiko said. The Duke looked apoplectic as Michiko continued, "The supposition, then, is that Duke Wrexham staged the kidnapping. But if he did, why would Puck be in on the plan? He hated Wrexham."

"But we have an answer," Beth said. "Duke Wrexham, I'm sure you remember your former chief chef?"

With that, a tall, awkward-looking faerie soldier stumbled up. With a blink, Beth removed Gregor's makeshift seeming. "Um…good morning, Duke?" Aloysius said.

"Since he left your employment," Michiko said, "he's been here on Earth, working in an Emigre cafe. The same one where Puck has breakfast every Sunday."

"Now since Puck was kidnapped and rescued," Beth said, "his behavior has changed. Besides hanging out with someone he used to actively dislike, he was cold and mean-spirited to his friends. But there was another change. Aloysius?"

"Yes?"

"Before the kidnapping, what did Puck eat for breakfast every Sunday?"

"The Flaming Pits of Hades omelet," the chef said. "With extra jalapenos."

"Enough!" Puck shouted. "What does this—"

"She's not finished!" Michiko screamed with a smile. Caught by surprise, Puck fell silent.

"Thanks," Beth said. "Now, Aloysius, what did Puck have for breakfast yesterday?"

"A Belgian waffle," he said. "With whipped cream and blueberries."

"And he finished it?"

"All of it."

"You are a ridiculous little fool, girl," Puck said, glaring scornfully at Beth. "So I decided to eat something different for breakfast. Why are you treating that like a major revelation?"

"Because I know the real Puck well enough to know that he's allergic to blueberries." Beth smiled from ear to ear. "You're not Puck."

He screamed and took one step towards Beth. She reared back and threw open her purse. "Gregor!" she shouted. "Now!" Gregor popped out of the bag and spoke three words in an ancient tongue. Puck fell to the ground, writing in agony. As he did, he started to change, to grow.

"He's a shapeshifter," Michiko said. "He and Duke Wrexham plotted together to get the Duke his revenge on Puck, and help him with his plan to take over the Hoblands. They kidnapped the real Puck."

"What happened to him?" Aloysius asked.

"Gregor's spell," Beth said. "It's forcing the shapeshifter back into his natural form."

As she finished, the shapeshifter rose, all traces of Puck gone. He was hairless, with teal green skin, the barest hint of ears and nose, and oversized, cruel black eyes. He glared at Michiko and Beth but said nothing.

Wrexham walked up to him. "This—this is just another seeming!" he said, smiling unconvincingly. "A trick by the Monkey Queen and the hobgoblins! This is why—"

The shapeshifter grabbed Wrexham. "I grow tired of your prattling, Duke," he said with a sneer. He hurled the faerie into Cantwick and his men nearby, sending them sprawling.

He spun to face Michiko. "As for you, Monkey Queen, if you ever want to see your friend again, you'll have to catch me." He turned and ran. Michiko sprinted after him, with Robyn hot on her heels.

Beth followed after them, trying desperately to keep the others in sight. She dashed out of the plaza and into an alley where she saw a black door-shaped shadow at the far end. As she watched, the shapeshifter stepped into it. "A porth," Beth said as Michiko and Robyn chased him through.

"Girl," Gregor said, "you do know this may be a trap."

"I know," Beth said. "It couldn't be any more obvious if there was a big neon sign saying 'trap here'. But Michiko may need your help, and someone has to carry you." She swallowed hard and walked into the porth.

Chapter Eleven

Aloysius had activated his seeming and slipped away in the chaos following the shapeshifter's unmasking. He made his way across the plaza, where the others were waiting. "What word?" asked Scylla, who was now wearing black robes over armor, with a sword at her side. Mandy and Mec were next to her; Windsor was off to the side, keeping watch.

"It's not good." Aloysius sighed, his seeming disappearing. "Michiko was right, but the whatever it was that was pretending to be Puck ran off, and she went after him with Beth, Gregor and Robyn."

"And the Duke?"

"Still planning on opening the auldgate to the Hoblands."

"All right. We need to figure out how—"

"Scylla!" Windsor said. He pointed; the others could see someone running off into the distance, fiddling with his belt. "Hobgoblin."

"What is he doing here?" Mandy asked.

"No good," Mec said. He pointed behind a bench.

They hurried over and saw what the hobgoblin had left there. It was a round bronze sphere adorned with spikes and wires. It was glowing. "What is that thing?" Windsor asked.

"Whatever it is, it looks…wrong. And frightening." Mandy shivered.

"It should." Mec looked back at the others. "It's a hobgoblin bomb."

"Oh Lords and Ladies." Mandy paled.

Scylla scowled. "That must have been Krexx. He must have heard about the invasion and thought this would stop it."

Mec was already taking tools from his belt. "Scylla, I'll need a protective sphere around me and the bomb," he said. "With an airhole, please, but set it to seal if the bomb goes off." The faerie gestured and narrowed her eyes, and the air around Mec and the bomb began to shimmer and solidify.

"Be careful, sweetie," Mandy said.

"I'll try, but the problem is, hobgoblin bombs are unstable." Mec's voice echoed inside the shield as he eyed the device. "Even the makers don't know when they'll go off or how powerful they'll be, due to the mechanical components not always being compatible with the magical ones. And it looks like this was thrown together quickly, so it'll be even more unstable."

"So that means…" Windsor said.

"It could take out just the plaza, or the town and the surrounding woods, or everything in a fifty mile radius." The gremlin knelt in front of the bomb. "And it could detonate any minute now, so let's hope that this is set to go off later, rather than sooner."

"Can you defuse it?"

Mec pried a panel off with the blade of a screwdriver. "I'm pretty sure I can. I'd feel a lot more comfortable if you guys were somewhere safe, though."

"Where?" Mandy asked.

"Try Los Angeles." Mec lowered his goggles and started to work.

Beth sighed with relief as she stepped through the porth without being assaulted. She saw the lightpath at her feet and whispered, "Gregor, stay down. There could be more shadow rooks." Gregor nodded as Beth closed the purse and started down the passageway.

She followed the lightpath silently, glancing around in the darkness, trying not to jump at every echo. After what felt like a century, she finally caught up with Michiko and Robyn. "There you are!" Michiko said.

"We seem to have a problem," Robyn said. She pointed down at the ground, and Beth saw that the lightpath ended a few yards away from them.

"So," Michiko said, "did anyone bring a flashlight?"

"I've got two." Beth dug into her jacket pocket; as she did, her purse slid down her arm.

A long, snaky tail suddenly slithered out of the darkness and coiled around Michiko's arms and torso, quickly tightening. Her staff flew out of her hand, hitting Beth's arm and sliding to the floor; Beth winced as her purse slipped off her arm. Michiko struggled against the tail, but it lifted her up and whipped her around before slamming her to the ground. She lay face down and still.

The shapeshifter emerged from the shadows. His new form was half-humanoid, with a long, thin but muscular snake-like tail replacing his lower torso and legs. He unwound his tail from Michiko's limp form and smiled cruelly.

"Michiko!" Beth screamed, running towards her. Before she could get to her partner, the shapeshifter backhanded her in her stomach. Beth fell to her knees, gasping in pain.

Robyn raised her sword and took a step towards the shapeshifter. "I would recommend against that," he said. He snapped his fingers, and two ogres stepped from the shadows and flanked him. "My mistress wants all of you alive, but I may not feel the same way. Drop your weapon now, or the humans die here."

With a look of disgust, Robyn laid her sword on the ground and stepped back. As she did, her foot bumped into Beth's purse; she instinctively kicked it back and away.

The shapeshifter picked up Michiko and threw her over his shoulder. "You two each escort one of the women," he said to the ogres. As one grabbed Robyn and the other lifted Beth, he added, "Bring their weapons."

The ogre carrying Robyn picked up her sword. The other bent and tried to lift Michiko's staff. "It's too heavy," he said, grunting from the effort.

"Weakling!" The other ogre chortled. "It's just wood!"

The shapeshifter walked over and tried to lift the staff. Despite his efforts, it stuck as if it had been welded to the ground. "Leave it, then," he said. He set off back into the dark, the ogres following with their captives.

Windsor had gone to search the plaza for other hobgoblin bombs. Scylla was concentrating on maintaining the shield around Mec. Mandy chewed her knuckle nervously, tears rimming her eyes. Aloysius was behind her, trying his best to comfort her.

As they watched, Mec carefully reached inside the bomb with a pair of tweezers. He slowly lifted a glowing orange gem out. He yanked a small glass containment jar from his belt, popped the hinged lid open and gently set the gem inside. He closed the lid and spoke softly; the lid sealed in place.

The bomb stopped glowing.

"All clear," Mec said with a smile as he started to put his tools away. The protective sphere vanished.

"That's it?" Aloysius said.

"That's it." Mec stood up and wiped his hands on his jeans. "We're all safe." Aloysius sighed and wiped his brow. Mandy ran over to Mec and hugged him.

"Thank you for not blowing us up, Mec," Windsor said as he rejoined the others.

"My pleasure," the gremlin said as he picked up the deactivated bomb. "See anything?"

"I did. It's not another bomb, but it's still not good."

"The auldgate's open?" Scylla asked.

"Not yet," Windsor said, "but from what I could hear, it won't be long. And a half-dozen of Wrexham's elite guard are surrounding the wizards."

"So getting to them would be a bit difficult."

"It may be getting worse," Aloysius said. "Look." He pointed at a group of patrolling faerie soldiers. They had seen him and the others, and were marching towards them.

Mandy gulped. "I thought you meant the other soldiers coming up behind us." She pointed to another patrol.

"Can I go back to bed now?" Aloysius asked.

"Robyn?" Beth said. "I think she's coming around."

Michiko groaned and shook her head. "Did anyone get the number of that aircraft carrier?" she said.

"Are you all right?" Robyn asked.

"I think so." Michiko started to stand, but dropped back to her knees. She looked down and saw the shackles on her wrists and ankles.

Beth rattled her shackles. "They weren't taking any chances." Next to her, Robyn, also shackled, nodded.

"This isn't a good thing, is it?"

"No."

"So what happened?"

"The shapeshifter ambushed us," Robyn said. "He knocked you out, then threatened you and Beth if I didn't surrender."

"And," Beth said, "he had two ogres with him. I think one of them was the ogre you rescued me from the night we met."

"Sunshine?" Michiko asked.

"Pardon?" Robyn blinked.

"Private joke," Beth said. The faerie nodded.

Michiko glanced around the room. It was small and was being used for storage, with bedding and cleaning supplies scattered about. There were two doors on opposite walls. "Any idea where those doors go?" she asked.

"No," Robyn said. "We've seen the shapeshifter and the ogres going back and forth."

"How did we get in?"

"The porth is behind you," Beth said.

"Where's my staff?"

"It's back through the porth. No one could lift it, so they left it behind."

"Okay," Michiko said. "Where's Gregor?"

"Don't you remember?" Beth said. "We left him with the others, so he could try to keep Wrexham from opening the auldgate to the Hoblands." Robyn nodded furiously.

Michiko raised an eyebrow. Then, she asked, "So, which door goes to the bathroom? I...I really need to pee." She blushed.

"You too?" Beth said.

"Dibs on the bathroom!"

"Well, I didn't need to go," Robyn said, "until you two mentioned it!" Michiko laughed.

"I'm giving them five minutes," Beth said. "Then, I'm going in one of those buckets." Michiko laughed again, and Robyn smiled slightly.

One of the doors flew open. The shapeshifter, back in his human form, strode in. "You're awake, Monkey Queen!" he said. "That's good news. My mistress is waiting." He smiled cruelly.

"Halt!" the patrol leader said. "State your names and purpose."

"No archers?" Scylla said. "How fortunate. Mandy? Do you remember what Michiko told you to do?"

The pixie nodded and exchanged nervous smiles with Mec. Then, she spread her wings and took to the sky.

The faerie soldiers stared at her for a moment. Then, they turned and advanced on Scylla. "Gentlemen," she said. "Before you come any closer, a warning."

The soldiers stopped. "Good," Scylla said. "Now, you will notice that one of my companions is, to put it mildly, frightening. Another is a gremlin, and trust me, he has more tricks than he has sanity.

"The faerie next to me is Windsor. You may have heard of him. He's here on Earth because he's wanted in three houses for various crimes of property and propriety. But each of those houses wants the other two to make the first move, for no one in any of them wish to face him in a swordfight.

"I'm sure you've heard of me. I am Scylla. I'm the Emigre who the Dukes don't want to return. They fear me." She smiled and laid her hand on the hilt of her sword. "So should you."

The soldiers took a step back. Windsor started to draw his sword. The soldiers stepped back further. Aloysius cracked his knuckles. Mec brandished the deactivated bomb and cackled madly. The soldiers turned and ran.

"That worked," Mec said, lowering the bomb.

121

"Thank goodness," Aloysius said. "I was about to throw up."

"What now?" Windsor asked.

"We retreat," Scylla said, "and we hope that Michiko's plan B works."

The shapeshifter dragged the three woman, one at a time and not very gently, into the room opposite the doorway he had come in from. Michiko was the last one brought in, and when she was dropped off, she saw the two ogres who had helped the shapeshifter with the other women. "You're right, Beth!" she said. "It was him! Hiiii, Sunshine!" That ogre cringed and hid his face in his hands as the other laughed. "I think I'll call your friend Lollipops!" Michiko added; Sunshine laughed loudly as Lollipops growled.

The women were in front of a raised platform. A large, throne-like chair was set in the center, flanked by two lit braziers that cast shadows across the room. Tapestries decorated the walls, and elegant area rugs covered much of the plush carpeting. On a shelf against one wall were several vases and jars, and Robyn's sword.

The door opened again, and a woman walked in, leaving the door open. She had long, wavy black hair and a floor-length black dress that trailed behind her and seemed to drift and shift as she moved. Her eyes were dark and narrow. "Monkey Queen!" she said as she passed Michiko. "We meet at last."

"The pleasure's all yours, I'm sure," Michiko murmured.

"Such contempt!" the woman in black said. "Typical." She sat in the chair on the platform; as she did, the shapeshifter stood by her, near one of the braziers. "I am Muirin," she told the captives. "I am the mistress of shadows. I walk through them; I command them and give them life."

"Impressive!" Michiko said. "Do you do children's parties?"

Beth studied Muirin. "I know you," she said. "You tried to talk me out of working with Michiko at Wrexham's gala. You've been after me all this time."

"That's how she got in without an invitation," Michiko said. "The whole 'walking through shadows' part."

"She may also have created or summoned the shadow rooks," Robyn said.

"Including the one at my window Friday night," Beth said.

Michiko raised an eyebrow. "You saw that?"

"I peeked out of my bedroom," Beth said.

"Enough with the exposition!" the shapeshifter shouted.

"No, let them continue," Muirin said. "I'm enjoying it." She smiled smugly.

"I'm almost done, anyway," Michiko said. "It's not just that you've been trying to lure or capture Beth. You were behind Puck's kidnapping all along. You and the shapeshifter. And Wrexham fell for it.

"The only question left is why."

There was a loud knocking, over and over, on the front door of the old Victorian. Feng rushed down the stairs. threw the door open and saw Mandy standing there, holding a smartphone. "Hi," she said. "I'm sorry, I know it's early, but I need to speak to Grandmother Fox."

Feng sighed and started to close the door. "Wait! Wait!" Mandy pushed against the door. "You need to let me in! It's an emergency! Michiko sent me!"

Feng stopped. "Michiko?" he asked.

"Yes! She told me to come here! Please let me in!"

Feng sighed again and stepped back; Mandy slipped inside as Feng closed the door behind her. "Wait here," he said as he hurried up the stairs.

A minute later, Grandmother Fox, wearing white silk pajamas and matching bunny slippers, came down to the foyer. "Young lady," she said to Mandy, "I hope you have a good reason for making such a ruckus at such an early hour."

Mandy tapped the smartphone screen twice and held it up sideways, facing Grandmother Fox. "This time, I do," the pixie said as the video started.

"Grandmother Fox! Hiiii!" Michiko said on the smartphone screen. "It's me, Michiko! And you remember Beth!" To her right, Beth smiled and waved. "Listen," Michiko continued, "if you're getting this message, that means that there's a crisis, and I can't help because I'm trying to find Puck and deal with his kidnappers. We need your help."

Grandmother Fox watched the rest of the video grimly. "Thank you for showing this to me," she said to Mandy after it concluded. "I'll do what I can. Please go back and let your friends know." Mandy nodded as Grandmother Fox headed back up the stairs.

"Why?" Muirin chuckled. "Why is that so important to you, Monkey Queen?"

"Curiosity," Michiko said. "What do you want with Duke Wrexham? What's in it for you?"

Muirin rose from her chair. "We both know the True Millennium is coming. It will bring changes." She started to pace around the platform, gesturing as if she were lecturing her captives. "I see what will happen to Earth. Humanity is not able to handle the change. Governments collapse. Dictators and opportunists from Faerie and other worlds move in. Civilization as we know it is destroyed, wiped clean.

"One of the keys to stopping this is to weaken Faerie. Not just the Courts, but the Outlands as well. They must remain divided. I knew that Duke Wrexham sought to expand his lands, and I had heard that the hobgoblins could soon be a threat.

"In my travels, I had met a shapeshifter." Muirin stopped next to him and laid a hand on his shoulder. "I sent him to infiltrate Wrexham's court, and plant the idea in his head. It worked beautifully; soon, Wrexham and the hobgoblins will be at war."

"Not if we can help it." Robyn glared defiantly at the sorceress.

"Bold words," Muirin said, "from someone in your position."

"So you had the shapeshifter give Wrexham the idea to kidnap and replace Puck," Michiko said.

"Where is he?" Beth asked.

"Somewhere safe," Muirin said. "After all, I may need him later." Beth's heart jumped for joy when she heard that, though she hid it as well as she could.

Michiko nodded. "So, what do you gain from this? If the hobgoblins are defeated, Wrexham grows stronger."

"Not in this case." Muirin resumed her pacing. "If Wrexham does destroy the hobgoblins, he will be openly scorned by the Outlands, and in all likelihood by some of the Dukes as well. But from what I have heard, the Hoblands have developed their defenses. The war will most likely result in both sides being crippled, and high casualties."

"'Casualties,'" Michiko said. "Including all the innocent lives that will be lost." There was a grim anger in her voice.

"They're just faeries and hobgoblins," Muirin said, with no emotion.

"Are you saying that their lives are worthless?"

"Less than human lives, yes. The lives I seek to protect."

"You're wrong, Muirin," Michiko said. "All lives matter. Non-human and human matter just the same."

Muirin's eyes flashed. "You are a fool to believe that, Monkey Queen. Humanity matters more than some greedy faeries and shiftless Emigres. And I will bring humanity through the times to come. I see the countries of Earth united. I see them driving away outsiders, and building a bright future. And the other worlds will leave us be."

"And I see you in the shadows," Michiko said. "You'll be running the show, won't you?"

"Who better?" Muirin smiled.

"What about the Emigres?" Beth asked. "What would you do with them?"

"The ones who work with me—" Muirin gestured to the shapeshifter and the ogres. "—will be richly compensated. The rest will be sent back to their homes, unless they resist."

"But some of them were exiled here!" Beth said. "If they're sent back, they'll be killed! Doesn't that matter to you?"

"Not in the slightest. Earth will be saved. That is all that matters."

"I refuse to believe that," Michiko said. "We'll find a way to keep Earth safe, and it won't lead to any blood being spilled."

"You're a fool for believing that," Muirin said. "You and your Grandmother Fox, and the Council of Eight."

She stopped pacing and looked down at the captives. "Beth McGill." Beth jerked her head up as Muirin said, "I would like to make you an offer."

"Lord Wrexham?" the faerie said as he nervously approached the Duke. "There are reports of intruders."

The Duke turned. "Is it the Monkey Queen, Lodge?"

"No, but—"

"Then get rid of them. We don't need anyone else getting in the way."

"My liege? If I may?" Lodge asked.

"Go ahead."

"Well, some of the men are on edge. They've heard about what happened with Puck."

"Just another trick of the Monkey Queen and her allies," Wrexham said.

"And they're reporting seeing a mad gremlin and a purple monster."

"All tricks with seemings."

"And they say that Scylla's here." Lodge gulped. "With Windsor."

"Really?" Wrexham forced a chuckle. "And are we to be scared of them?"

"Arguably."

"Let them try to stop us." He pointed to where the wizards were performing their ritual. "Any minute now, the auldgate will open. The Hoblands will be mine. And the Monkey Queen—"

"My liege?" Lodge said.

Wrexham sighed. "More intruders?"

"You could say that." Lodge pointed up.

The sky directly above them grew dark. A woman, dressed in white and standing fifty feet tall, hovered in the clouds. Lightning flashed in her eyes.

"Duke Wrexham of Faerie!" she thundered. "I am Grandmother Fox, of the Council of Eight! It has come to my attention that you are using the Earth as a springboard for an invasion! Earth is not your plaything or your battleground!"

She gestured. A burst of pure white light struck the ground where the wizards were standing, knocking them back like bowling pins. The light then sank into the ground between them. "The auldgate to the Hoblands is sealed again," Grandmother Fox said. "It will never be reopened."

Wrexham reached for his sword, but shouted with pain and yanked his hand away. He could see his men dropping their weapons. "You and your men are no longer welcome here," Grandmother Fox said. "Abandon all your plans to attack the hobgoblins and leave Earth at once."

"My liege?" Lodge asked. Around them, faeries panicked, running about madly or standing still with shock and fear.

Wrexham shook his head. "The invasion is off," he said, gritting his teeth. "We're returning to Faerie. Give the order to retreat." Lodge nodded and hurried away.

Grandmother Fox watched as the faerie forces made their way out of the plaza, putting on their seemings and heading for the auldgate in the woods. Wrexham was in the last group to leave. "Duke? One more thing," she said.

"Yes?" he said.

"The Monkey Queen sends her regards." Grandmother Fox smiled and vanished.

Duke Wrexham cursed all the way to the auldgate.

"What?" Beth said.

"It's very simple," Muirin said. "Like almost everyone, I am fooled by seemings. I have tried time and again to find a way to see through them, without success. Until I can conquer this weakness, I could fall victim to anyone in a disguise.

"Join me, Beth. Let's work together to save Earth's future."

Beth looked up at Muirin and said nothing. Michiko stared quietly at the floor. "Beth!" Robyn shouted. "Don't do it! Don't—" Before she could finish, the shapeshifter walked over to her and swatted her hard on the head. She fell silent, glaring at the shapeshifter.

"If you accept my offer," Muirin said. "I'll let Puck go, alive and unharmed."

Beth remained quiet, but her thoughts were racing. She felt like there was no other choice; they were outnumbered and chained, with no way out. She could feel the fear, the hopelessness, building up in her.

Muirin sighed. "All right. I will also release the Monkey Queen and the faerie, alive and unharmed. And that is my final offer."

Beth swallowed hard. "No," she said.

Muirin reared back. "What?" she shouted.

"No." Beth looked the sorceress in the eye. "What you plan is wrong. Your future is going to be built on the blood of Emigres, of your enemies, of innocents. And I won't have their blood on my hands."

The shapeshifter grabbed Beth's hair and yanked her head back; she gasped in pain as he pushed his face into hers. "Don't be a fool!" he said. "If you turn her down, you won't leave here alive! She only needs your eyes!"

"Enough," Muirin said. The shapeshifter released Beth and moved back by the brazier. "I'll give you one last chance. You and your friends will not leave this place alive…unless you agree to work for me."

Beth squeezed her eyes shut. "Michiko…Robyn, Professor…I'm sorry," she whispered. "But the answer's still no." The despair she had been fighting swelled up, wrapping around her heart. She hung her head as a tear trickled down her cheek.

"Beth." She jerked her head up and looked at Michiko, who was staring calmly at her. "Listen to me," she said. "We're all going to get out of here, and we're all going to be fine. I promise."

The passageway was, for a brief moment, flooded with brilliant white light.

The flare quickly faded, leaving behind a pile of straps, gold fabric, and sequins. A guinea pig crawled out of the wreckage that had been Beth's purse, coughing and shaking his head as he pushed sequins aside.

Gregor had been stunned when the purse had been dropped and then kicked away during the ambush. As he tried to clear his head, he cursed the Monkey Queen, the unseen enemies who had left him abandoned there, the crisis he had found himself in, and his reincarnated lot in life. But, above all else, he cursed the purse.

When he had finished the last swear word, he looked up and down the passageway. "Beth?" he asked. "Monkey Queen?" There was no answer. Gregor started to swear again, but stopped when he heard a clatter echoing through the passageway.

He turned and saw Michiko's staff. It slowly rose several inches above the ground, fell down with a thud, lay still for several seconds, rose again, fell again. A gleam of understanding shone in the guinea pig's eyes.

Gregor hurried over and stopped in front of the staff as it set down. He waited through another rise and fall cycle. As it hit the ground again, he jumped on one end, his paws scrabbling for a toe-hold.

The staff slowly rose again, hovering in mid-air, moving very slightly as if it were testing its load. Gregor wrapped his legs around it and gritted his teeth. Then, the staff shot down the trail, Gregor clinging on to it like an awkward witch as it rocketed towards the porth.

Muirin's mocking laughter filled the room. "Such bravado, Monkey Queen!" she said. "You're helpless! You're at my mercy! And you say you'll keep the others safe!" She laughed again.

"I will. And you'll regret threatening and kidnapping my friends." There was confidence, and a hint of anger, in Michiko's voice.

"And how are you going to accomplish that, you little fool? You're outnumbered! You're in chains!"

"Well..." Michiko paused. "I have two things that you don't."

"Show me, then." Muirin folded her arms.

"Okay. They should be here in just a moment." The Monkey Queen smiled.

Her staff flew through the doorway into the room and struck Muirin in the head. She fell to her knees, dazed but conscious, as the staff landed with a clatter. The shapeshifter and the ogres gaped, frozen in place by shock.

Beth turned her head towards the doorway. "Gregor!" she shouted as she saw the guinea pig. He spoke two words, and the shackles that held her popped open; she saw Robyn kicking hers away.

Michiko jumped up, her shackles dropping off. "Beth, take cover," she said as she leaped over her and Robyn. Her staff flew into her hand as she landed in front of the ogres; she swung it and hit Lollipops hard on the head. Sunshine growled, but before he could act, Michiko spun and kicked him in a very painful place. As they both crumpled, she somersaulted high in the air.

"Hey, ugly!" the Monkey Queen shouted as she landed next to the shapeshifter. "Time for round two!" She decked him before he could react. As he reeled, she swung her staff and caught him in the midsection; he flew three feet through the air and smashed into the wall. He landed on his feet, his face contorted with fury, but he winced in pain as he kept his distance from Michiko.

"Stop them!" Muirin shouted. The ogres started to get to their feet. As they did, Beth saw, through the gap between them, the shelf with the vases and Robyn's sword.

Beth swallowed and dashed between Sunshine and Lollipops. She stopped at the shelf and grabbed the sword by the hilt. "Brave but foolish," Sunshine said as he turned towards Beth. "You don't know what to do with a sword."

"Actually, I do," Beth said as she dropped to one knee. Fighting off nerves, she aimed the sword between the two ogres and tossed it past them; it bounced twice and landed in front of Robyn.

"Thank you, Beth." Robyn picked up her sword as the ogres turned to face her. "Now...two against one?" she continued with a smile. "That hardly seems fair. Would you two like to go get some help to even the odds a bit?" The ogres growled and charged the faerie.

Beth crouched down beside the shelf, watching the chaos, trying to stay out of danger. Then, she heard a voice say, in a tone that made her shudder, "Defy me, will you?"

She looked up and gasped as she saw saw Muirin on the platform, majestic and terrible as the darkness embraced her. "You first," the sorceress said, raising a shadow-wreathed hand. "The Monkey Queen should never have—"

"You're forgetting someone, girl."

Muirin spun and saw Gregor, standing by the edge of the platform. "Oh, this is rich," she said. "I'm being challenged by a hamster now!" She chuckled as she pulled her arm back.

"Guinea pig!" Gregor said. He then muttered under his breath. The shadows in Muirin's hand exploded in a blast of light, with a force strong enough to send her sprawling.

Beth took a quick glance around the room. The ogres were pressing Robyn, but had to stay out of range of her sword. Gregor watched Muirin, waiting for her next move. The shapeshifter was circling Michiko, ducking back as she jabbed with her staff. "Whenever you're ready," Michiko said.

Robyn swung at Sunshine, who had managed to get in close, and cut through his tunic, just missing his chest. She left herself open for Lollipops, who threw a left hook. Robyn dodged it, but stumbled, and Sunshine pushed her down. Gloating, he raised a huge fist.

Beth knew that if the ogres could defeat Robyn, she would be next, then Michiko. She glanced around and saw all the vases and jars on the shelf next to her. *It kind of worked before*, she thought; she grabbed a jar, spun and threw it at Sunshine's head. It shattered, and he winced and bent over. Robyn jumped to her feet and kicked the ogre hard in the knee; he yelped in pain and fell.

Muirin, fury twisting her face, flung a writhing shadow at Gregor. He dissipated it with a word and a flash of light. "I know about you!" she shouted. "You had true power! Why are you working with these fools?"

"Wandering through Limbo for a thousand years can change you!" the guinea pig said. He tensed as more shadows gathered, but then he and Muirin both stopped as they heard a loud thud.

The shapeshifter had switched back to his half-snake shape and had caught Michiko in his tail. He had thrown her to the ground, but she was prepared and rolled as she landed, dropping her staff. She came up quickly to her feet, but the shapeshifter was quicker; he wrapped his tail around her torso and right arm, and began to squeeze. "You—could have just—asked for a date," Michiko gasped.

"I'll get more pleasure from seeing you die," the shapeshifter said. Muirin laughed.

Beth stepped out from behind the shelf and grabbed a small urn. "Put that down, you idiot!" Muirin shouted. "Do you have any idea how valuable that is?"

"Really?" Beth said. "Here! Catch!" She tossed the urn at Muirin, but the throw went to the sorceress' right; she had to dive to get it. That was what Beth had wanted. She grabbed the heaviest vase and, with the way cleared, threw it with all her strength at the shapeshifter's head. It shattered against his skull; he shouted with pain and loosened his grip on Michiko. "That's for Puck!" Beth yelled.

The Monkey Queen worked her free arm into her pocket and pulled out a plastic kitchen squeeze bottle filled with a red liquid. She popped the cap off with her thumb and sprayed the contents on the shapeshifter's face. He screamed and reverted to his humanoid form, releasing Michiko. "Gotcha!" she said as she picked up her staff.

"What...?" Muirin said, dumbstruck.

"Michiko had told me that shapeshifters have to adopt a weakness before they can master a new form," Beth said. "When we realized what we were facing, we knew right away what its weakness was—spicy food. It wouldn't have left such an obvious clue otherwise."

"So I whipped this up especially for him, with three different kinds of hot sauce," Michiko said. "Plus plenty of spices, some jalapenos, and an aged habanero or two."

Muirin cursed as she sprung to her feet, pointing at Beth. A flash of light drove her back down to her knees. "Thanks, Gregor!" Beth said.

The shapeshifter looked at Michiko with murder in his eyes. "I'll kill you!" he screamed, charging at her. "You disgusting, verminous, little—"

"Still got half the bot-tle!" Michiko said in a sing-song voice, and as she spoke, she squirted the remaining contents into the shapeshifter's open mouth.

He shrieked and fell to the floor, clutching his throat and gagging, trying to spit out Michiko's concoction. Unable to control himself, he shifted into his half-snake form, his tail whipping about blindly. It caught the brazier and knocked it over. Blazing coals struck the floor, the tapestries and Muirin's chair, and fires started to burn.

"Ogres! To me!" Muirin shouted as she knelt by the shapeshifter. The ogres, who had been losing their combat with Robyn, eagerly broke away and hurried to the sorceress' side. Shadows began to envelop them.

"Monkey Queen!" Muirin said as the shadows grew. "This is not the end. Even if you should escape, I will find all of you and destroy you."

"Send me a postcard!" Michiko said with a wave as the shadows began to contract. In a moment, they were gone, and so were Muirin and her hirelings.

Michiko spun to face the others. "Robyn, take Gregor and search the other rooms. Beth, check this room for seemings and hiding places. I'll watch the porth. And be fast—that fire won't wait for us."

In a few minutes, they had all gathered in the storage room. "Anything?" Michiko asked.

Beth shook her head. "The living room is clean. Robyn?"

"Nothing," said the faerie. "The other rooms were sleeping quarters for the ogres. They were filthy."

"There was also a laboratory," Gregor said. "Some of the things in there…let them burn, I say."

"So, no Puck." Michiko scowled. "Time to go, then."

"But he's got to be here!" Beth said. "Where else would he be?"

"I don't know, but we can't stay here. It's not just the fire. Look." Michiko pointed at the porth.

"It's that shadow witch," Gregor said. "She somehow tapped into faerie magic to create that porth and cross into others. Without her around, it's starting to shrink. It'll be gone soon."

"Beth," Michiko said, "we'll do everything we can to find Puck. But we need to get out of here first, and this is the only way out."

Beth nodded sadly. "I'll take Gregor," she said. Robyn handed her the guinea pig, and the group stepped into the porth.

They hurried through the darkness, heading for the lightpath. Michiko was several steps ahead of the others, keeping watch out for trouble. Robyn brought up the rear, staying close to Beth and Gregor. "What happened here?" the faerie asked as they passed a pile of sequins and shredded fabric on the floor not far from where the lightpath started.

"Revenge," Gregor said.

Beth glanced at what used to be her purse, and the darkness beyond it. She blinked and gasped. "Robyn!" she shouted. "Take Gregor and get out!" She handed the surprised guinea pig to the equally surprised faerie and ran into the darkness.

As she ran, she began to doubt what she saw. *It could be me seeing things,* she thought. *It could be Muirin's last trick.* But then she blinked again, and she reached for her flashlight, and she saw that she wasn't wrong.

It was Puck. He was bound hand and foot and gagged, but looked to be in good shape.

"Professor!" Beth said, smiling. He looked at her and urgently shook his head, trying to speak through the gag.

"Forget it," she said as she bent down and grabbed his forearms. "I went through a lot to find you, and I'm not leaving you here." She started to drag Puck back towards the lightpath.

After a minute, her head bumped into something. She realized that it was the top of the passageway; it was shrinking around them. She gritted her teeth and crouched down further, pulling Puck as fast as she could go.

It wasn't enough. By the time they had reached the lightpath she was nearly bent over double, gasping for breath. "Professor?" she said. "If...if we don't make it out of here, I'm sorry. I—"

Then Beth felt an arm around her waist, lifting her like a sack of potatoes. She saw Puck being lifted the same way. For a moment, the passageway was a blur around them.

Then the Monkey Queen, crouching as she ran and carrying Beth and Puck under her arms, burst out of the porth and into the alley. She slid to a stop on her knees, setting her friends down gently, as the porth collapsed behind them.

Chapter Twelve

The sun was coming up, and Beth could see that Robyn and Gregor were there. So were Mec, with cutters in hand, and the others from the plaza; the gremlin went right to work on Puck's ropes. "How did you know?" Beth asked Michiko, who was helping her up.

"Robyn told me what you did," Michiko said. "There was only one reason you'd do something like that."

"Something dumb, you mean," Beth said. "I'm glad you came back for me."

"Glad to do it. Just don't scare me like that again!" Michiko said with mock sternness.

"I'll try not to." Beth smiled. "Oh, and Michiko? Thanks." Michiko smiled back and nodded.

Mec had cut Puck free, and Mandy had brought him a bottle of water. "How are you, sir?" Aloysius asked.

Puck finished the bottle. "Aloysius, I am tired, hungry, sore, and happier than I've been in ages. There were times I thought I would never see any of you again." He smiled and started to stand.

"Be careful, sir," Aloysius said. "We should get you a doctor."

"It can wait." Puck turned towards Robyn and clasped her hand. "My goddaughter...the words fail me. Thank you, with all my heart." Robyn nodded and smiled, blinking back a tear.

Puck then walked unsteadily over to Michiko and Beth. "Quite an adventure, lass," he said to Beth, laying a hand on her shoulder. Beth smiled as she wiped her eyes.

"Michiko," he then said to the Monkey Queen, "I owe my life to you and Beth. I thank you both, again with all my heart." She blushed and looked down, smiling.

Robyn set Gregor down, took Puck's arm, and led him away. They passed Mandy and Scylla as the Emigres walked over to Michiko. "Here's your smartphone," Mandy said, handing it over.

"Thanks," Michiko said. "Did you have to use it?"

"Yeah. She was there in a minute. Sealed the auldgate and everything. It was cool."

"And I missed it?" Michiko pouted.

"Check your phone later," Mandy said with a smile.

"Really? Thanks! Any other problems?"

"Just Krexx dropping by with a hobgoblin bomb," Scylla said.

Michiko grimaced and slapped her forehead. "Fill me in later," she said as Puck and Robyn rejoined them.

"I have managed to convince Robyn," Puck said, "that the best thing for my health and well-being would be a breakfast or two. Aloysius, perhaps you'd consider opening early today?"

"It's his day off—" Mandy started to say.

"Not a problem, sir!" Aloysius said. "I'm sure Clyde will be glad you're back."

"Excellent! Robyn, you'll like the food there. Everyone?"

"Michiko and I will be along in a minute, Professor," Beth told him. He raised an eyebrow and nodded, then headed off with the others, leaving Michiko and Beth alone.

"Michiko..." Beth pulled her thoughts together. "I...I've made my decision."

"You're having pancakes for breakfast?" Michiko asked with a half-smile.

"Well…I do want a short stack on the side," Beth said. "But that wasn't what I meant."

"I know." Michiko's smile faded as she looked away. "Beth…it's been great working with you. You've been a big help, especially back there with the shapeshifter. Thanks." Beth blushed as Michiko continued, "I'm really really hoping you'll stay around, but we both know how dangerous things got. I'll understand if you don't want to be my partner." For a moment, Beth could see the sadness in her eyes.

"Yeah, it did get pretty scary," Beth said. "But the thing is, you didn't mention how much fun it would be. Or how good it would feel to help people who needed it. And what it meant to do something with myself besides studying and watching TV."

"There are some things people have to discover for themselves," Michiko said, looking back at Beth.

"Grandmother Fox again?"

"Yeah."

Beth nodded. "She was right. But I've made up my mind."

Michiko tensed up. "Okay," she said, fidgeting and biting her lip.

Beth took a deep breath. "Michiko…I'm in."

"You are?" Michiko's eyes widened.

"Yeah." Beth finally let out the smile she'd been holding in. "I'll help you save the world. Partner."

"Yaaay!" Michiko grinned happily and grabbed Beth, giving her a big hug. This time, Beth was ready for it and hugged back. As she did, she heard Michiko say, "Beth?"

"Yeah?"

"Thank you," Michiko said very quietly. Beth's smile widened, and she squeezed Michiko a little bit tighter.

"Ahem." They looked down and saw Gregor, watching them impatiently. "All done?" he said.

"Gregor!" Michiko bent down, picked up the guinea pig, and gave him a peck on the cheek. He made a face.

"Thank you, Gregor," Beth said. "You were amazing."

"It was nothing," he said. "Oh, and I'm not sorry about your purse."

"Neither am I. Breakfast?"

"Yes. And after that, now that all this is done, do I get to go back to the pet store?" Gregor said.

Michiko and Beth looked at each other, smiled, then looked at Gregor. "No!" they shouted at the same time, as they started running to catch up with the others.

Thanks for reading! Want more? We hope so!

To get the latest Monkey Queen release news, background info and cheesy gossip, just sign up for our mailing list at eepurl.com/XXmlv . We promise that your email address will never be sold, given away or forced to eat pickled sea slug.

You can also:

Like us on Facebook at www.facebook.com/monkeyqueenbooks

Check out our blog at http://monkeyqueenbooks.blogspot.com/

Follow us on Twitter at @monkeyqueenbks

Acknowledgments

Many thanks to Willow for the wonderful job she did on the front cover! If you like her work as much as I do, you can check out her gallery at willow-san.deviantart.com, follow her for updates and more at www.facebook.com/willousan, and drop by http://society6.com/willowsan to shop at her webstore!

Thanks to Keri Knutson at Alchemy Book Covers for her fine design work! Find her at www.alchemybookcovers.com/

Thanks to Jason and Marina Anderson at Polgarus Studio for their great formatting work! Find them at www.polgarusstudio.com/

Thanks to Greg Espinoza. Sorry things didn't work out.

Thanks to brave beta reader Lyle Tucker. I may not have agreed with all your observations, but the ones I did agree with made this, I think, a better book.

Thanks to everyone who has encouraged me down this road over the last 30 or so years, and thanks to everyone who's created something that's inspired me to become a writer and create this story. I'll skip the detailed list because I'd leave someone out, and because it might end up being longer than this book.

And thanks to Adelle for all her support and encouragement.

About The Author

Robert Dahlen was born in the Quad Cities, but moved to California when he was three and a half years old. For many years, he described the high point of his life as being depicted as a "putrid little paper pusher" in an Adolescent Radioactive Black Belt Hamsters comic book; things have thankfully improved since then. He lives in Northern California with a tablet stuffed with e-books and works in progress, shelves of books and graphic novels, lots of penguins, and a nice hat. He is hopefully working on another Monkey Queen book even as you read this. (Oh, and it's pronounced "duh-LANE", as in "The rain in Spain falls mainly on Dahlen," which wouldn't make any sense even if he had been to Spain, which he hasn't.)

Printed in Great Britain
by Amazon